Emily stared at Leandro in mute silence. She didn't want him to carry on—she really didn't want to hear what he had to say on a subject she had no desire to talk about—but she felt like a rabbit frozen in the headlights while a car moved inexorably at full speed towards it.

'Ah, I see you get where I'm coming from.'

He sat up and his hand snaked up to her wrist, tugging her down beside him so that she half fell onto the rug before shuffling into a sitting position whilst glaring impotently at him.

'The cat is out of the bag, Emily. You're no longer a personal assistant hiding behind a bland exterior with a non-existent private life.'

She was so close to him that he could see the flicker in her eyes...he could almost *smell* the scent of an awareness she was desperate to conceal.

'You're engaged to be married to a man for whom you have...feelings of...what, exactly? Certainly not love and—let's be honest here—definitely not physical attraction. And do you know how I've come to that conclusion?'

He ran his thumb along the side of her cheek in a gesture that was shockingly intimate and she pulled away sharply.

'Point proved,   my dear personal as   me...'

Cathy Williams is originally from Trinidad, but has lived in England for a number of years. She currently has a house in Warwickshire, which she shares with her husband, Richard, her three daughters, Charlotte, Olivia and Emma, and their pet cat, Salem. She adores writing romantic fiction, and would love one of her girls to become a writer—although at the moment she is happy enough if they do their homework and agree not to bicker with one another!

Recent titles by the same author:

SECRETS OF A RUTHLESS TYCOON
ENTRALLED BY MORETTI
HIS TEMPORARY MISTRESS
A DEAL WITH DI CAPUA

Did you know these are also available as eBooks?
Visit www.millsandboon.co.uk

THE ARGENTINIAN'S DEMAND

BY
CATHY WILLIAMS

Published in Great Britain 2014
by Mills & Boon, an imprint of Harlequin (UK) Limited,
Eton House, 18-24 Paradise Road, Richmond, Surrey, TW9 1SR

© 2014 Cathy Williams

ISBN: 978-0-263-90885-5

Harlequin (UK) Limited's policy is to use papers that are natural,
renewable and recyclable products and made from wood grown in
sustainable forests. The logging and manufacturing processes conform
to the legal environmental regulations of the country of origin.

Printed and bound in Great Britain
by Blackprint CPI, Barcelona

THE
ARGENTINIAN'S
DEMAND

CHAPTER ONE

Emily Edison stared resolutely ahead of her as the elevator purred upwards to the twentieth floor, disgorging employees along the way. It was the morning rush at Piccadilly Circus, in the towering glass building where she worked in the heart of London. She rarely experienced this because she rarely came to work later than eight in the morning, but today…

Slim fingers tightened on the neat leather satchel at her side. Inside the bag her letter of resignation felt like an incendiary device, waiting to explode the minute it was released from its fragile containment. When she tried to imagine how her boss would take this she felt slightly sick.

Leandro Perez was not going to be happy. When she had begun working for him over a year and a half ago he had already been through countless secretaries, the most successful of whom had barely lasted a fortnight. Change, in this instance, was *not* going to be as good as a rest…

'They take one look at him,' his long-suffering and fairly elderly PA had told her, two days after her arrival at the company, 'and something unfortunate happens to their brains. But you, thank God, seem to be made of sterner stuff. When I told Leandro that I would stay until I found a successful replacement I had no idea I would still be here after six and a half months…'

Emily had taken to the job like a duck to water. Theoretically, at the age of twenty-seven, she was still young enough to be susceptible to having her brains scrambled by a man who could turn heads from several blocks away, but he did nothing for her. His outrageous good-looks left her cold. The deep, rich velvet of his voice with that ever so slight sexy Argentinian accent did not put her off her stride. When he strode round her desk to look over her shoulder at something on her computer her nervous system remained perfectly stable and functioning. She was, as had been predicted by his previous PA, made of far sterner stuff.

But right now, riding the elevator by herself, because the last employee had scuttled through the doors somewhere around floor ten, she felt queasy with nerves even though she asked herself…at the end of the day, what could he do? Throw her through the window? Condemn her to immediate exile somewhere on the other side of the world? Threaten to lock her up and throw away the key?

No. The most he could do would be to get very, very annoyed—and annoyed he most certainly would be…especially considering that only a fortnight ago he had given her a glowing appraisal and a correspondingly glowing pay rise, for which she had been immensely grateful.

She inhaled deeply as the lift doors opened and she emerged onto the opulent directors' floor of the wildly successful electronics company her boss owned and ran with ruthless efficiency.

It was just one of his wildly successful companies. They ranged from publications to telecommunications and he had recently, for a little light relief, begun a programme of investment into boutique hotels in far-flung places. Such was the vastness of his wealth that he could weather any sluggish profits he made from that venture—although, if the first three hotels were anything to go by, he would yet again discover that he had the Midas touch.

She would miss all this, she thought, looking around at the busy department. Plants and artfully arranged smoked glass partitions maintained a certain amount of privacy for the various secretaries who helped keep the machinery ticking over. Several waved at her.

She would miss the occasional lunch with them in the office canteen. She would miss the stunning surroundings of a building which was a tourist attraction in its own right. She would miss the adrenaline-fuelled pace of her work, its diversity, and all her responsibilities—which had increased a hundredfold since she had started.

And would she miss Leandro?

For a few seconds she paused and frowned towards the thickly carpeted corridor that led to his massive office suite.

Her heart picked up pace. She might not have drooled over him, the way some of the other girls did, but she was not completely immune to his impact. She was in full possession of twenty-twenty vision and she would have had to be blind not to be aware of just how sinfully sexy the man was. The fact that he represented everything she despised didn't detract from that unassailable truth.

And, yes, she confessed to herself, she would most certainly miss working with him. He was nothing if not a challenging employer—indeed, the most brilliant, energetic, vibrant and demanding man she had ever worked for.

Before she could get carried away on that tangent, she refocused her mind, pursed her lips and smoothed her skirt with shaky hands. As always, she was dressed like the ultimate professional. Charcoal-grey pencil skirt, sheer flesh-coloured tights, black court shoes, a crisp white blouse and the matching charcoal-grey jacket that completed the suit. All this despite the fact that it was June and the weather was heating up with every passing day. Her pale blonde hair was neatly coiled in a bun of sorts, out of harm's way.

She strode confidently towards Leandro's office, pausing en route to dump her satchel and her briefcase on her desk, which was in her own private outer office, before knocking on the interconnecting door.

Behind the door, Leandro glanced up from his computer and then pushed himself away from the desk. This was a first. His secretary was late, and he was disconcerted to find that he had wasted far too much time wondering what was keeping her. The fact of the matter was it wasn't even nine yet. Her working day was not due to begin for…another ten minutes.

'You're late,' was the first thing he said as soon as she had entered his office.

On cue, his midnight-black eyes swept over her, taking in the prim suit, the even primmer blouse, the severely restrained blonde hair. She was as cool as an ice maiden. Very little ruffled her feathers, and when she looked at him she did so without the slightest flicker of interest. There were times, in fact, when he almost suspected that she might not even like him very much—although he invariably put that down to the workings of his imagination.

Women liked him. That, he conceded without a trace of vanity, was a given. He assumed that it was due to a combination of the way he looked and the reserves he had in his bank account. Money and a halfway decent appearance were almost always a guarantee of lively interest from the opposite sex.

'Technically,' Emily told him calmly, 'I'm not even due in for another eight minutes.'

She looked at her boss, seeing him in a different light now that she knew she would soon be on the way out. She would hand him her letter of resignation just before she left for the day, and thus spare herself the full force of his anger.

He really was, she thought with a detached eye, a thing of great beauty. Black hair was swept back from a face of chiselled perfection. He had lashes most women would have killed for. And there was a lazy, shrewd, perceptive depth to his dark eyes that could, she knew, be at once disturbing and exciting. There had been instances when she had caught him looking at her with a mixture of mild curiosity and lazy masculine appreciation, and for all her toughened resistance she had been able to see just what it was about him that had women drooling.

He was tall—at least four inches taller than her, and she wasn't petite at five foot eleven—and even in a suit, it required very little imagination to guess at the muscular physique underneath.

Oh, yes, he had the full package—and it drove women nuts. She knew because she had full access to his private life. She chose gifts for his women—five and counting over the past year and a half. She ordered elaborate bouquets of flowers when, sadly, their time was up and he was ready to move on to a new model. She fielded his women's calls and, on one memorable occasion, had had to handle a personal appearance at the company.

He invariably dated obviously sexy women. Curvaceous, dark-haired beauties with big breasts and come-hither eyes. The sort of women who always commanded far more male interest than any skinny supermodel ever could.

Involvement in his personal life was *not* something she was going to miss, and it reminded her of why, despite the stunning good looks, the agile brain, the sharp acumen, and those flashes of wit that could bring a grin to the most poker-faced of spinster aunts, she still didn't like the man.

Leandro frowned but decided to let it go, even though

her cool response had carried just a hint of rebellion behind it.

'And might I expect this to become a habit?' he enquired with raised eyebrows. He pushed himself away from his desk and relaxed back in his chair with his hands folded behind his head. 'If it does, then some advance warning would be appreciated. Although…' he allowed a few seconds of silence '…considering the amount you're paid, you might find my tolerance of your clock-watching a little limited.'

'I won't be clock-watching. I never do. Shall I bring you a refill for your coffee? And if you let me know what you want done about the due diligence on the Reynolds deal I can get started…'

For the rest of the day, however, Emily *did* watch the clock—something she never had in the past—and with each passing minute her nerves became a little more stretched.

Was she doing the right thing? It was a big step. Handing in her notice would signal an end to her substantial salary, but what choice did she have?

At a little before five-thirty, with her resignation letter burning a hole in her bag, she debated her options. Of course she had options. Who didn't? But when you got right down to it all her options aside from the one she was going to take now led to the same dead end.

She cleared her desk with the feeling that she was looking at it for the last time. He would certainly ask her to leave immediately. For starters, she was privy to confidential information. Would she have to sign some sort of disclaimer? It sounded like the sort of thing that might happen in a B-rated movie, but who knew? When it came to business, Leandro was not a man to take any chances.

He glanced up briefly as she entered the office, took in

the very obvious fact that she was dressed to go and point-edly looked at his watch.

'It's five-twenty-five...' Emily forestalled any sarcasm '...and I'm afraid I have some...stuff to do this evening...'

She normally worked until after six—sometimes far later if there was a lot to get through.

'I've completed all those emails you needed to be sent to the lawyers in Hong Kong and forwarded them to you for checking. You'll find them in your inbox...' She hovered, reached into her bag and withdrew her resignation letter. 'There's just one more thing...'

Leandro picked up the uneven tenor in her voice and stiffened. He looked at her narrowly and indicated the chair facing his desk. 'Sit.'

'I'd rather not. As I said, I'm in a bit of a rush...'

'What's going on?'

It was more of a demand than a question. Today was proving to be full of surprises—at least as far as his sec-retary was concerned. Kicking off with her late arrival at work, she had spent the day in a state of mild distraction, jumping when he happened to come up behind her so that he could review something on her computer, working with the ferocious absorption of someone intent on pretending that there was no one else in the office, and barely able to meet his eye when addressed.

All of those minute changes were so under the radar that he knew they would have passed unnoticed by anyone other than himself, but his antenna was sharp when it came to detecting nuances—especially nuances in a woman with whom he had spent the past eighteen months working in close quarters. She was his secretary, but he had, in actual fact, spent a hell of a lot more time with her than he ever had with any of the women he had taken to his bed.

So...what was going on?

Leandro was intrigued, and what startled him was the acknowledgement that he had actually been intrigued by her for a long time. Intrigued by her aloofness, her detachment, her almost pathological desire for privacy. Intrigued because she was the only woman he had ever met who barely reacted to his presence.

She did her work with the highest level of efficiency, and even when they had worked late on several occasions, and he had ordered in a takeout to keep them going, she had politely refused to be drawn into any form of personal conversation, preferring to keep everything on a professional footing. Chinese food, chopsticks and no downtime. Instead intelligent discussion of whatever deal they had been working on, with her notes spread next to her on the desk.

'What do you mean?'

'I mean, Emily, that you've been acting strangely all day...'

'Have I? I've managed to complete all the tasks you've set me.'

She sat, simply because he kept staring at her and remaining on her feet felt oddly uncomfortable. She had planned on handing him her letter of resignation and leaving perhaps before he could even open it. It now looked as though that option would be removed from her.

Now that she was on her way out—now that she knew she would never clap eyes on him again—she was oddly aware of his potent masculinity. It was almost as though she had now given herself permission to look at him—*really look at him*—without the barrier of her inherent scorn for the type of man he was standing in the way, acting as blinkers.

Something dark and forbidden raced through her, making the hairs on the back of her neck stand on end. Those dark eyes were so...so brooding...so intense...

She looked down quickly, angry with herself and wondering where that sudden powerful awareness had come from. Surreptitiously she extracted the letter from the satchel and licked her lips.

'You're not a performing seal.' Leandro relaxed back into the leather chair and looked at her. 'There's more to your job than simply completing the tasks set. Granted, you're not the most open book in the world, but something's definitely off with you today. You've been acting like a cat on a hot tin roof and I want to know why. It's impossible to work if the atmosphere in the office isn't right.'

He picked up his fountain pen—an expensive present from his mother, who firmly believed that letters were still written and technology and computers were simply a passing phase. He twirled it idly between his fingers and Emily watched, guiltily mesmerised by the movement of his long fingers.

'Perhaps,' she said in a stilted voice, 'this might go some way to explaining my behaviour. Not that I've noticed anything amiss. I've done my job as efficiently today as I always have done.'

Performing seal? Was that how he saw her? As someone who came in, did what she was expected to do to the very highest standard, but lacked in all personality? Dull? Boring? An automaton? She had kept her distance and had kept her opinions to herself. Since when had that been a crime? Her mouth tightened and she swallowed back an intense temptation to tell him just what she thought of him.

Leandro looked at the white envelope in her hand and then looked at her.

'And that is…?'

'Take it. Read it. We can discuss it in the morning.'

She made to rise and was told to sit back down.

'If a discussion is warranted, then we'll have the discussion right here and right now.'

He reached for the envelope, slit it open and read the brief letter several times.

Emily schooled her features into a mask of polite detachment, but she had to unclench her hands and her heart was racing—beating so fast that she felt it might burst through her ribcage.

'What the hell is this?'

He tossed the letter across the desk in her direction and Emily snatched it before it could flutter to the ground. She smoothed it on her lap, staring at the jumble of words. Granted, it was a very brief letter of resignation. It said that she had enjoyed her time working with him but felt that the time had come for her to move in another direction. It could not have been more dry or unemotional.

'You know what it is. It's self-explanatory. It's my letter of resignation.'

'You've had fun and now it's time to move on…am I reading it correctly?'

'That's what it says.'

'Sorry. Not buying it.'

Leandro was shocked. He hadn't seen this coming and he was furious at what he saw as inadequate advance warning. Furthermore, *he* was the one who generally decided when one of his employees was ready to be shown the door. He had had enough experience of simpering young girls batting their eyelashes and getting into an annoying flap every time he looked at them and asked them to do something simple.

'If I remember correctly, you had a substantial pay rise recently, which you very happily accepted, and you informed me at the time that you were perfectly satisfied with the working conditions here.'

'Yes. I...I...hadn't thought about resigning at that point in time.'

'And yet less than a month later you have? Did you have a sudden revelation? I'm curious. Or have you been looking for a replacement job all along and just biding your time until the right one came your way?'

The thought of another endless series of airheads was not a pleasant one. Emily Edison had been the perfect secretary. Intelligent, unflappable, always willing to go beyond the call of duty. He was used to her. The thought of getting in to work and not having her there at hand was inconceivable.

Had he taken advantage of her? Of her quiet efficiency? Her willingness always to go the extra mile? He rejected any such notion before it had had time to take root. He *paid* for her to be willing to go beyond the call of duty. He was pretty sure that she would be hard pressed to find another job as secretary in the heart of London where the pay equalled what she got.

'Well?' he prompted. 'Has someone made you an offer you can't refuse? Because if that's the case, consider whatever offer you were tempted by doubled.'

'You would *do* that?'

Her mouth fell open. Performing seal she might very well be, but he valued her, and although she knew that through a process of intelligent deduction, it was gratifying to hear it put so starkly into words.

'We work well together,' Leandro said bluntly. 'And I expect that I am sometimes not the easiest man in the world to work for...'

Expecting a standard negative response to that statement, he was disconcerted when it failed to be delivered.

'Is that it?' he asked, leaning forward with frowning intensity. 'Have you got a gripe against *me*...?'

He couldn't quite conceal the incredulity in his voice

and Emily, for the first time, looked at him with cynical directness. Of course never in a million years would Leandro Perez *ever* think that *any* woman wouldn't be one hundred per cent happy to be in his presence. She might have bucked the trend by *not* being one in that long line of women who swooned the second those dark, intense eyes settled on them, but even so he would *still* assume that he had an effect on her because that was just the sort of man he was.

A player. Someone so inherently aware of his massive pulling power that it would be just inconceivable that it might not work on *some* women.

'I haven't got a gripe against *you*,' Emily said slowly.

She felt a thrill of recklessness, because right now, at this very moment in time, she was permitted to speak her mind. By tomorrow afternoon she would have cleared her desk and would have disappeared from here for good, with no need for references from him—although she knew instinctively that they would be very good, because he was, for all his faults, scrupulously fair.

Leandro tilted his head to one side and kept his eyes firmly fixed on her face. Her colour was up. Was she *blushing*? He hadn't associated her with such a girlish reaction. She was always so self-possessed…and yet…

His dark eyes drifted down to her mouth. She had full, soft lips, and even if they had registered somewhere in his subconscious before now he certainly felt as though he was seeing them for the first time. Perhaps she had shed that ice-cold image, because there were cracks in it now, through which he wanted to pry, find out what lay underneath.

Emily sensed the shift in his attention—from boss trying to uncover the reasons for her sudden unexpected resignation to boss looking at her with *masculine interest*.

Her skin tingled. She felt as though she was in the grip of an acute attack of pins and needles.

'No?' Leandro drawled. 'Because your expression is telling a different story.'

Emily, so accustomed to being the dutiful impeccable secretary in his presence—the secretary who never allowed her personal feelings to tip over into the work arena—stiffened.

'If you must know, I've never enjoyed having to do your dirty work for you.'

'Come again?'

She couldn't quite believe that she had just said what she had. The blood rushed to her head and she knew that she was as red as a beetroot. Gone was the frozen, aloof façade she had kept up for the past year and a half.

She looked at him with defiance and took a deep, steadying breath. 'Presents for those women you no longer had any use for…goodbye gifts you couldn't even be bothered to choose…arranging opera tickets and theatre tickets… booking expensive restaurants for women I knew I would be sending those goodbye gifts to in a few weeks' time… That should never have been part of my secretarial duties…'

'I don't believe I'm hearing this.'

'That's because you're not accustomed to anyone telling you anything you don't want to hear.'

Leandro released a long, sharp breath and sat back to look at her. Her face was alive with genuine, sincere emotion. She was leaning forward in the chair, and of their own accord his eyes drifted down to the prissy top.

He wondered what she looked like underneath it—wondered what it would feel like to make love to his icy secretary who was now in the act of revealing the sort of passion that could make any red-blooded man burn. He wondered what that hair would be like let loose. Hell, he didn't even know how long her hair *was*! His intense curiosity extinguished any anger he might have felt at what she had just said. At any rate, it was certainly true that he wasn't accustomed to being criticised.

'So you didn't like your involvement in my personal life?' he murmured.

'Maybe Marjorie was accustomed to doing stuff like that, but I feel you should have established whether *I* would mind...'

'I guess if you felt so strongly about it you should have said something earlier...'

Emily blushed, because he was absolutely right. And why hadn't she? Because she had needed the money and she had been keen not to put a foot wrong.

'There's nothing more annoying than a martyr who puts up with the unacceptable and only says her piece when she's handed in her resignation...which brings me back to the *why*...'

'Well, like I said, I feel it's time to move on... I realise you will probably want me to leave immediately, so I thought I could just pack my things up and be done in a day...'

'Leave immediately? What gives you that idea?'

'What do you mean?' Emily asked in some consternation. 'Of *course* you want me to leave immediately. You don't see the point of employees hanging around once they've handed in their notice. I remember quite clearly you saying that they need to be removed from sensitive information, and also that their demotivation can spread like a virus...'

In actual fact she had only known of a couple of instances of employees handing in their notice. Pregnancy and emigration being the reasons. Mostly people stayed

with the company because the pay was second to none—
as were the working conditions.

'Marjorie stayed on for quite a while before she finally
left…that seems to fly in the face of your *sensitive information* theory…'

'Yes, but…'

She looked at his raised eyebrows, the slight tilt of his
head, and for a second she wondered whether he was just
toying with her.

'My responsibilities have been far greater.' She stumbled
over her words as she contemplated the prospect of working out her notice having told him in no uncertain terms
what she thought of certain aspects of her job…

'True,' Leandro agreed.

He allowed the silence to thicken and deepen. *Immediate departure? Why?*

'And you're telling me this because…?'

'Why would you want me around if you think I'm an
annoying martyr?'

Emily took a different approach, but Leandro Perez was
not a man who could be browbeaten, and even as she tried
a different ruse she felt the sinking sensation of knowing that her departure would not be going quite accord-
ing to schedule. She had been short-sighted, had dropped
her mask, and now she would be stuck for at least another
month with their boss-secretary relationship not on the safe
footing on which it had always rested.

'You have a month's notice to work out,' Leandro informed her flatly. 'You've lost your mind if you imagine
that you're going to leave me in the lurch with a string
of unsuitable candidates turning my working life upside
down.'

And he was honest enough to admit to himself that it
rankled…the fact that she had been happy to jump ship

without a backward glance when she must have known that he depended on her! What the hell had ever happened to *a sense of responsibility*?

He offered her an expression of thoughtful contemplation and politely waited for her to try and find a few more pointless excuses.

Emily envisaged one long month of interviewing prospective candidates for a guy who would almost certainly reject all of her choices. She had handed in her notice and he wasn't going to make life easy for her. And now that she had been foolish enough to actually tell him what she thought about his antics involving the opposite sex...

No, life was not going to be a walk in the park at all over the next four weeks.

'But of course you *do* have a point,' he mused, resuming the light tapping of his fountain pen on his desk. 'You *have* assumed far greater responsibilities than Marjorie ever did. She always maintained that she was hanging on to new technology by the skin of her teeth whilst knowing very well that there was no way I would ever get rid of her because of her length of service. She worked for my father in Argentina. Did you know that?'

'She didn't mention it.'

'She was over there on holiday after university and looking for temporary work so that she could improve her Spanish. She applied for an office job at my father's company and he liked her. Said she had spirit. He employed her on the spot, and as things turned out she fell in love with a local guy, married him and remained working for my father until eventually she and her husband moved over here years ago so that she could be close to her family.

'Two of her daughters married English guys and now live here as well. When she moved she came as a package deal to me, but in truth her heart was never in the upward climb. She did a damn good job, but you…' He relaxed back and folded his hands behind his head. 'You're quick…you're professional…you never need to be told anything twice…'

Emily accepted the flattery with as composed a demeanour as she could muster and reminded herself that it came with the massive downside of being asked to work out her notice. But the pleasure of being complimented so elaborately brought colour to her cheeks.

'Which is why I can't afford to lose you immediately, and also why you were rewarded with so much responsibility…so much confidential information on clients… For all I know—' he sat forward suddenly, taking her by surprise '—you could be moving on to one of my competitors… Who knows? You're a closed book, Emily…'

'Moving on to one of our competitors…?'

Leandro raised his eyebrows at that unconscious slip of the tongue, but he didn't relax his posture, and nor did he come even close to cracking a smile.

'Are you being *serious,* Leandro?'

Somehow she had managed to avoid using his name for the majority of her time working with him and it felt strange on her tongue. She was catapulted back to that odd sensation she'd had earlier, when she had suddenly and inexplicably become *aware* of him—aware of his startling sexuality, aware of the dragging power of his personality when work was not the issue at hand.

'I'm always serious when it comes to work.' Leandro, still leaning forward with his elbows splayed on the desk, was looking at her very carefully. 'As you might have gathered by now, I'm not a man who takes chances when it comes to my companies…'

'I get that—but I would *never* disclose anything confidential to anyone!'

'Better safe than sorry, though, wouldn't you say…?'

Would she even miss him?, he thought, enraged with himself for even thinking it.

'I'll get in touch with the agency first thing in the morning.'

Distractedly she thought that a person could get lost in those dark eyes of his, which were resting on her with lazy, brooding speculation, and then she mentally slapped herself on the wrist for letting her imagination get the better of her.

Not only was it foolish but it was entirely inappropriate, given the current circumstances.

'No need just yet...'

Whoever said that a good head for business precluded a talent for creative thinking?

'I have a project that's coming to an end on a small island in the Caribbean. Finishing touches to one of my hotels before the grand opening in six weeks' time. I need to be there personally to sign off on the details...'

Not strictly true, but it would certainly serve his purpose at this juncture. No way she was going to just up sticks and disappear into the sunset without a backward glance. Furthermore, she intrigued him—and now, with this peculiar letter of resignation, she was intriguing him even more.

'That's not a problem. I'm more than capable of covering in your absence, and of course I will communicate daily on email. I can even begin sifting through prospective replacements so when you return you only have to interview the handful I've selected...'

'Not precisely what I had in mind. I *do* have to keep an eye on you—as you have so aptly brought to my attention... So here are my thoughts: you and I will travel to my hotel and test-drive it, so to speak. Make sure the nuts and bolts are all in place, the paperwork is spotless, the teams are ready for when the place opens... And, of course, out there you will be removed from any temptation to get in touch with anyone who might be interested in buying sensitive information and it will give me time to get my people to firewall anything that could be stolen... What do you think? No, scratch that. Just get your passport, pack a suitcase and book two first class tickets for us to leave first thing in the morning. Much more fun than sifting through potential candidates for a job, wouldn't you agree?'

Emily blanched. 'What sort of timescale are we talking about?' she asked faintly.

There seemed little point in taking issue with his implication that she might be a common thief. His suspicious nature had helped get him where he was today, and it was as ingrained in his personality as an icy wasteland was in hers.

'Well, you *do* have to give me a month's notice... I imagine a fortnight should suffice when it comes to overseeing the final touches of the hotel...'

'*Two weeks?*'

'You sound shocked. I know you have a passport, so where's the problem?'

'I'm sorry, but I'm not going to be able to do that.'

'And that would be because...?'

'Because I have certain commitments.'

'And would these "commitments" be related to that letter of resignation you produced an hour ago?'

'Yes.'

Emily drew a deep breath and looked away. She could feel curiosity emanating from him in waves. Leandro Perez had a brilliant and enquiring mind. Was he about to let her go without trying to delve into the precise reasons for her resignation? How naive she had been to imagine that that might have been the case.

'I'm all ears—because I'm still paying your salary and asking nothing that breaches the bounds of your duty.'

'I realise that. It's just that…that…'

'That what?'

'I'll be leaving London. I'm getting married…'

CHAPTER TWO

FOR A FEW seconds Leandro wondered whether he had heard correctly. *Getting married*? It was as ludicrous as if she had suddenly announced that she was resigning so that she could fulfil a lifelong ambition to climb backwards up Mount Everest. No, it was even more ludicrous—because never, not once, not for a passing moment, had she intimated that she had any kind of social life. She might very well have kept her personal life to herself, but there wasn't a woman on the face of the earth who could resist letting slip something as big as *that*.

Furthermore, where was the diamond rock she should be wearing on her finger?

'I'm not buying it,' he said.

'I beg your pardon?'

'You heard me, Emily. I'm not buying it.'

'How…how *dare* you?'

A tidal wave of pure red rushed through her head. The cool, aloof persona—the one that was her constant companion—vanished under the force of her anger. Anger that he had the nerve to think she was lying. Anger at the implied insult that she was just so dull, so boring, that it was inconceivable anyone might want to marry her. Anger that he just couldn't believe she wasn't one of those simpering girls who would not have been able to resist the compulsion to blab to her boss about a fiancé in the wings.

The sheer arrogance of the man was unbelievable. But why did that come as any great surprise? Hadn't she witnessed first-hand just how arrogant he was in his dealings with women? Hadn't she seen for herself how he treated them? Like playthings to be picked up and then dumped the second their novelty value wore off.

Memories of the past and her own experiences of someone with that same lethal power to destroy hurtled towards her like a rocket with deadly cargo, and she deflected its impact with a little less than her usual practised ease.

'How dare I what?'

'How dare you presume to know anything about me?' Emily bristled. 'Just because I haven't mentioned my private life, it does not give you the right to assume that nothing goes on in it!'

'I'm curious as to the whereabouts of this fiancé of yours when we have spent hours working until all hours of the night—which, incidentally, wasn't that long ago. In fact… if my memory serves me right…three weeks ago we had a run of several Chinese takeout nights when that Dutch deal was on the verge of completion. I can't imagine any testosterone-fuelled young man wanting his woman cooped up with her boss into the early hours of the morning… Or maybe those late lie-ins I gave you made up for the inconvenience…?'

He appeared to give this some thought and then shook his head slowly, his dark eyes fixed on her face all the time as his curiosity bloomed into a driving, unstoppable need to *know more*.

'No…' he drawled. 'You've never had any problem with unsocial hours. That would have featured on the menu had this fiancé been on the scene. So…how long has it been going on?'

'That's none of your business,' Emily said through stiff lips.

'I'm making it my business,' he responded coolly, 'in light of the fact that it appears to be influencing your ability to do your job.'

'It's not influencing *anything*…'

'You've already informed me that you have a problem accompanying me to the Caribbean to oversee the end of this project. I'd term that as *influencing your ability to do your job*… Look, Emily…' He sighed and raked his fingers through his dark hair. 'We've been working together for almost two years. We've had an excellent working partnership—aside, of course, from your simmering resentment about the way I conduct my love-life…'

And where, he wondered, had *that* come from? Poor experiences in the past with some guy who broke her heart?

'Is it just so damned inconceivable that I might have a passing interest in something as groundbreaking as your engagement? Forget the fact that you're going to leave me in the lurch…'

'I have no intention of leaving you in the lurch. I shall make sure I find a suitable replacement.'

He noticed the way she had clumsily tried to evade his question. Fascinating.

'Leaving that aside for the moment, how long have you been going out with this mystery man? What's his name, anyway?'

'Are these questions still in line with the fact that you're *not buying* what I've told you?'

'I'm mystified by the lack of an engagement ring on your finger,' Leandro said mildly. 'Perhaps you took it off this morning when you were washing the dishes, but I feel certain I would have remembered seeing it before…'

'I'm not a great believer in engagement rings,' Emily mumbled uncomfortably.

'And yet there must be romance and passion there if you don't feel comfortable travelling with me for a fortnight to wrap this hotel business up…'

He had never seen her like this before. Her hectic colour brought a liveliness to her face that was captivating. She looked like a different woman. Still beautiful, but animated now, no longer with that impassive mask designed to keep the world at arm's length.

He had never been into blondes, but interest was kicking in. He wondered whether that was because the lines between their professional relationship and the personal were beginning to blur. Hell, what an inappropriate reaction! The woman had just announced that she was about to tie the knot with some guy and here he was, assessing her in ways he had never done before and allowing his imagination to break its leash and take up residence in entirely unacceptable fantasies that involved him getting down and personal with this new, intriguing creature squirming in front of him.

'His name is Oliver,' Emily admitted reluctantly, steering the conversation away from all talk about romance and passion.

The mere notion of those foreign emotions was enough to make her lips curl with cynicism. Romance? Passion? Why not throw love into the mix while he was about it?

Leandro detected the shadow that crossed her face, the way her full lips tightened fractionally. He had never really known what was going on in his secretary's head and he wondered idly whether she knew just how much of a challenging gauntlet she was throwing down in her evasiveness.

For someone like him—someone to whom women had always been prepared to bare their souls, whatever his response, indeed, who would have been prepared to do anything to net his interest—her obvious reluctance to divulge even the most innocuous of facts about her situation was a compelling reason for him to keep pushing.

Thinking about his varied and changeable love-life made him distractedly recall that fleeting, gone-in-a-heartbeat expression that had crossed her face at the mention of romance and…what else was it he had said…? *Passion*.

Was this mysterious fiancé less an object of passion than a…a last resort guy? Underneath that controlled exterior, was she just plain scared of ending up on the shelf? Or maybe some experience of someone who hurt her had left her wary of romance? Was that it?

The questions raced through his head and he didn't bother to fight his curiosity in chasing answers.

A fortnight in the Caribbean, aside from allowing him to be personally on hand to make sure the project was launched smoothly, promised to be an interesting experience.

'Oliver… Oliver what…?'

'You wouldn't have heard of him.'

'The expression *pulling teeth* springs to mind…'

'Camp,' Emily said through gritted teeth. 'His name is Oliver Camp.'

'And Oliver Camp would object to your accompanying me on a business trip, would he?'

'I'll come.'

Arrangements might have to be put back a few weeks, but in the long run that would make little difference. They were both keen to tie the knot and get the whole thing over and done with, but sometimes Fate threw a spanner in the works, and in this instance the spanner came in the form of a very large, very muscular and hellishly dynamic guy who effectively had her in his pocket.

At any rate, arguing with him would, in the end, be counter-productive. She had never known him to give anything up without a fight—and a winning fight at that.

'Wonderful news! So glad you've come round to the idea...'

He glanced at his watch and stood up, and Emily reluctantly found herself surreptitiously following the economical fluid movement of his long body. She seemed to have stored up remembered images of him, so that she felt almost familiar with the sight of his strong forearms sprinkled with dark hair, the way he unrolled the sleeves of his white shirt, the length of his fingers...

It alarmed her, and she looked away hurriedly and followed suit, standing up as well.

'I trust you'll make all the necessary arrangements first thing in the morning?' He strolled towards the door and slipped on his jacket.

'Are you leaving work already?' Emily directed the question to his broad back and he looked at her over his shoulder.

'So it would appear.'

He *never* left work before seven. Even when his diary was free of all meetings or conference calls, as she knew it was now.

'How come?' she found herself asking, and instantly regretted her impulsive question.

What on earth was wrong with her? Had some crazy recklessness been unleashed inside her? Was it all downhill from here on in? She had another month of his company! Was she going to work that month trying to put a brake on whatever nonsense her mouth decided to come out with? All her reserve seemed to be unravelling.

'Come again?' His dark eyes roved over her flushed face and he raised his eyebrows.

'I apologise. Of course it's none of my business when you decide to leave the office. I just thought… I wondered… You usually take the opportunity to consolidate stuff after normal working hours when the phones aren't ringing quite so much…'

Leandro turned fully to face her and leant indolently against the wall. 'You're flustered.'

Was that designed to make her feel even more hot and bothered? If so, it worked. She could feel heat tingling in her cheeks. 'I'm not at all flustered,' she lied. 'I'm merely… merely…'

'Demonstrating a perfectly natural human curiosity as to an alteration in my usual routine?'

'It's…'

'Absolutely none of your business.' Leandro shrewdly nailed what she had been about to say again—that the time he chose to walk out of his office was not a matter she was entitled to question. 'However, as you appear to be in such a rush to leave…for whatever "stuff" you claim you have to do…' He invited a response to this prompt and was unsurprised when none was forthcoming. He shrugged. 'I thought I'd call it a day. At any rate, there are things I need to do if I'm to be out of the country for a couple of weeks…'

Emily lowered her eyes. He was currently without a woman. She had dispatched the last hapless member of his harem several weeks previously. The poor woman had not had a very long run, although in fairness her brief appearance in his life had certainly been an expensive one, and she had left the better for several expensive items of jewellery and a red moped which she'd claimed matched her preferred choice of nail colour and was essential for getting around London.

So was there another waiting in the wings? She felt the familiar antipathy towards his life choices rise up into her throat like bile. She knew she shouldn't. People lived their lives the way they chose to live them, and she should be indifferent and non-judgemental, and yet…

Leandro continued to look at her. He felt as though he were seeing her in 3D for the very first time. At least partially in 3D. Certainly he realised that her pose was very familiar to him, although it had always been one to which he had paid next to no attention. Whenever he had casually asked her to buy a parting gift for a woman she had always lowered her eyes in very much the same way as she was doing now. Her mouth would purse and she would comply with whatever he asked without complaint, but, yes… in the light of what she had told him about her views on his love-life…

Disapproval was stamped on her face. It was running through her head that he was leaving early because he had a hot date with a woman. Leandro decided that he would give her all the freedom she wanted to imagine what she clearly considered the worst interpretation.

'Right. I'll see you in the morning, Emily. And…' He paused, just in case she thought that she might disappear without a backward glance and leave him high and dry. 'Don't even consider doing a vanishing act, because if you do I'll pursue you to the ends of the earth and take you to court for breach of contract. I've been an exemplary employer and I expect exemplary service in return—even if it's only for the duration of a month. Understood?'

'I wouldn't dream of vanishing.' But there would be some loose ends to tie up before she went away with him.

On her way back to the tiny bedsit she rented in South London, she contemplated those loose ends and was frustrated to discover that her mind wasn't completely on the task at hand.

In fact her wayward thoughts insisted on disappearing around corners, streaking off down blind alleys and generally refusing to be tied down. After that conversation with Leandro, which was *not* one she had predicted, she found that she couldn't quite get the man out of her head.

She unlocked her front door and realised that she didn't quite know where the commute had gone, because she had been so busy playing over that encounter in her head.

Now, looking around her ridiculously small bedsit, she grounded her thoughts by reminding herself that once this matter had been sorted, once this marriage was out of the way, she would no longer have to live in a place that was, frankly, a dump. The paint on the walls was peeling, there were signs of rising damp, and the heating system was so rudimentary that it was preferable to leave it off in winter and just make do with portable heaters.

She wondered what Leandro would think if he were ever to stray accidentally into this part of the world and into her cramped living quarters.

He would be horrified. On the salary she was paid she should have been able to afford somewhere more than half-way decent in a good part of London. But after her money was spent there was precious little left for life's small indulgences, such as passably comfortable living quarters…

She got on the phone to Oliver before she could begin to wind down, and he picked up on the second ring.

There would be a slight delay in their plans, she told him, and sighed wearily. She perched on the chair in the hall. It was so uncomfortable that she felt her landlord must have redirected it to the house when it had been on its way to the skip to be disposed of, because that was all it was good for.

In her head, she pictured Oliver. The same height as her,

fair hair, blue eyes—hardly changed at all from the boy of fifteen she had once dated for the laughably short period of three months, before exam fever had consumed her and before he and his family had sold their mansion and disappeared off to America. They had kept in touch sporadically, but even that had faded after his parents had died in an accident ten years previously.

'What sort of delay?'

She explained. Two weeks away, and then she would be back and they could progress. She knew that it was a delay barely worth writing home about, but she was desperate to get this whole thing wrapped up—although she made sure to keep that desperation out of her voice.

She spent the rest of the evening in a state of mild panic. Two weeks abroad with Leandro. Two weeks in the sun. Sunshine was synonymous with holidays, with relaxing, and yet she would be on tenterhooks the whole time, guarding herself against…

Against what…?

As she continued to tie up her loose ends—loose ends that *needed* to be securely tied up before she left—her mind continued to play with that suddenly persistent question.

Guarding against *what*…?

Unbidden, thoughts of Leandro floated past her walls of resistance, lodged themselves in her head. Thoughts of how he looked, the way he had stared at her with those dark, semi-slumbrous eyes, the soft, silky angle of his questions, the way their conversation had dipped into murky uncharted territory…

There had been no mention of what sort of clothes she should take. She vaguely knew the layout of the resort—knew that it comprised individual cabanas on the beach: sweet little one and two-bedroom huts that looked as though they had been there for time immemorial but which in fact were equipped to the highest possible standard and had only been standing for six months tops.

They formed a charming cluster in front of the main hotel, which itself was small and likewise very organically designed. There was a pool which mimicked a waterfall, plunging into a quirkily laid out lake, but each of the cabanas came with its own plunge pool anyway.

It was the height of luxury and, like it or not, she was not going to be able to pull off her usual uniform of starchy suits and sensible court shoes.

Swimsuits, shorts, sundresses. The sort of clothes she didn't possess. And she had neither the time nor the inclination to go out on a shopping spree.

The prospect of facing him the following morning was not a pleasant one, and she made sure to arrive, yet again, shortly before nine. If he interpreted that as some sort of restrained rebellion then so be it.

In fact she arrived to find a message on her desk telling her that he would be out for the day. Judging from the list of instructions for her, it seemed that he had hit the office even earlier than he normally did.

And the number one instruction was for her to sort out flights to the island. As if she were in any danger of forgetting it!

By five Emily was drained, and she was getting ready to leave when the phone rang and she was accosted by the dark timbre of his disembodied voice down the line.

How had she spent so long never being affected by that? How was it that his voice had never made her toes curl the way it was doing now?

In the act of putting on her jacket, she literally had to sit down and control her breathing as he demanded a debrief on the various things he had asked her to do. Had she sent those emails to the Hong Kong subsidiary of the electronics plant he was taking over…? Had she seen the response from the Briggs lawyers…? The Glasgow arm of his telecommunications outfit needed confirmation of price bands for new contracts and—could she make sure to hard copy all the relevant data by the morning…? And, last but not least, had she booked their flights.

Leandro relaxed back in his chauffeur-driven car. He had spent the day in a buoyant mood. He had one more company under his belt after some hard bargaining, and the following day…

Underneath his annoyance and frank bewilderment at Emily's decision to resign, his shock at the reason she had given and the uncomfortable sense of betrayal at her short notice and lack of forewarning, there was a tug of intense satisfaction at the prospect of them travelling to the Caribbean.

He had spent a lot of the day thinking of her. He had played over in his mind the conversation they had had, the changing expressions on her face. She had been…*shifty*. She had answered his questions when pushed, but he had been left with the feeling that her answers only skimmed the surface.

The fact that satisfying his curiosity would ultimately have no bearing on her departure was an irrelevance as far as Leandro was concerned. He got a kick just thinking about travelling down an unpredictable path for once when it came to the opposite sex.

Was he becoming jaded? It was a question he had never asked himself. He was thirty-two years old, in his prime, and he enjoyed a wide-ranging and satisfying love-life. Or so he had always imagined. Now he wondered whether it was quite as satisfying as he'd thought if he could find himself so taken over by the pleasurable novelty of discovering this untapped side of his secretary.

The last woman he had dated had faded from the scene three weeks previously and here he was, becoming *fixated* by this new vision of Emily Edison—an Emily Edison who was suddenly so much more than the sum total of her parts.

Hell, he had been *fantasising* about her! Wasn't that a little bizarre?

Had he reached a stage where novelty was so compelling? He had nothing against marriage, per se. He assumed he would marry eventually. Someone suitable. Someone from an equally wealthy background. He had had a narrow and salutary escape years ago, from a woman who had played the hard to get game to perfection. She had teased him for just the right length of time, convinced him of her shyness and her indifference to his money... Her real agenda had been uncovered only because he had happened to overhear a conversation she'd had on the phone to her mother...

So, sure, he would marry in due course—someone he knew was not after his money. His sisters were all married, after all, and his parents had had a long and satisfying marriage. He could enjoy the freedom of a bachelor life for as long as he wanted. But how satisfying, *exactly,* had that been of late?

He frowned and thought of the women who had cluttered his life over the years. Beautiful, sexy, compliant, always willing to fall in with whatever he wanted. On paper, it sounded good enough, but the reality of it was slightly different. His boredom threshold was narrowing with each passing relationship. The thrill of the chase had vanished a long time ago.

'The earliest flight I could get was for the day after tomorrow,' Emily said now with staccato crispness.

She wondered where he was now. Back at his apartment? In a restaurant waiting for some hot date? She didn't want to waste time taking any mental detours in search of such details.

'Time?'

She told him. Just vocalising the details of their flights brought home to her the reality of the trip.

'Take tomorrow off,' he said wryly. 'I expect you'll have all sorts of...*things* to do before we go...'

'That's fine.' Emily adopted her best businesslike voice. 'I'm sure there will be things that need completing on the work front before—'

'Emily,' he interrupted decisively, 'I'll be in before seven tomorrow morning. I'll make sure whatever needs doing gets done.'

'But won't you want me to take care of the work transfer? Get Ruth on board to field the correspondence...?'

'We're not travelling to the outer ends of the Amazonian rainforest,' he informed her. 'There will be an internet connection. The bulk of the correspondence will be dealt with by us. You can see it as work as usual bar a change of scenery.'

'Oh, good,' Emily breathed.

Instantly Leandro had to fight down a spurt of annoyance.

'Which doesn't mean,' he added, 'that I'm expecting you to pack your starchy suits and high-heeled shoes...'

'I *do* realise that that wouldn't be appropriate,' Emily snapped.

'The swimming pool will be up and functioning...'

Emily pretended not to hear that. 'Will you want me to meet you at the airport?'

'I'll send my driver for you. Or I can swing by your place and get you en route...'

'That won't be necessary!'

She shuddered at the thought of Leandro Perez seeing where she lived. If he were curious about her now, then he would certainly be collapsing under the weight of questions should he ever step foot in her house and see her sparse, substandard surroundings.

'And it won't be necessary for you to send your driver for me, Leandro. If you don't trust the public transport system, then I'm happy to get a taxi and charge it to the company.'

'Fine.' He banked down his irritation.

A fortnight in the Caribbean... Sure, there would be work to be done, but still...sun, sea and sand.

A driver to fetch her and her enthusiasm was nil. But then...

His mind swung back to the mystery fiancé about whom he knew nothing.

'So, what did...I forget his name...have to say about your trip abroad with the boss?' Leandro asked, smoothly diverting the conversation to a destination which spiked his curiosity. 'All hunky-dory with the time you're going to be spending with me?'

'Why shouldn't he be?'

Emily tried and failed to imagine the situation Leandro was hinting at...a jealous lover laying down ground rules, maybe phoning every hour on the hour just to make sure that nothing untoward was going on... And then she went hot at realising where her mind was heading.

She could virtually hear the sound of him shrugging nonchalantly down the end of the line.

How had they managed to travel to this place where their conversations led away from work onto treacherous quicksand? Where her grip was so uncertain? Even re-moved from his presence, in the sanctuary of her own office, she could feel herself burning as her blood thickened and her mouth dried up.

Her breasts felt suddenly heavy, her nipples tingly and sensitive, and a rush of pure shame flooded her. Whatever this door was that had opened up a crack between them, she was determined to shove herself against it as hard as she could until it was closed again.

'Well, if you're absolutely sure that you won't need me at work tomorrow…'

Leandro gritted his teeth as she once again skirted around the conversation he found he was keen to have. The eager, obliging and annoyingly forthcoming women he was used to had faded completely in their attractiveness. He marvelled that he had not become irritated with them before. Compared to Emily's sparing, guarded, tightly controlled boundaries, they now seemed utterly lacking in any sense of challenge.

And a good challenge had always been something he enjoyed getting his teeth into.

'Absolutely… Go out and have some retail therapy…'

'I don't do retail therapy,' Emily responded automatically.

'*All* women do retail therapy.'

'All the women *you* know do retail therapy. At any rate, I shall take the time to pack and…and…'

'And…?'

'There are a couple of things that I shall need to do before I leave… It's a long time to be out of the country…'

'A fortnight?'

Emily sighed. Leandro Perez was persistent. If he wanted to acquire something he acquired it—whatever obstacles got thrown in his way. It was just the way he was built. He had once told her in passing, over a meal delivered to his office courtesy of one of the top restaurants in

London because they had needed food after twelve hours of solid work on a thorny deal, that persistence was a gene he had inherited from his father.

'He taught me,' Leandro had said drily, 'that if you want something you have to go for it, and that the things you most want seldom drop into your lap like ripe fruit falling from a tree…'

Emily had inwardly sniggered. That being the case, he had clearly never really wanted any of the women he had dated, because one of the most stunningly predictable traits they had in common was their ability to fall like ripe fruit from a tree straight into his lap.

She had said with her customary politeness that sometimes you just had to give up on certain things because that was the wiser option, and had then immediately clammed up when he had tried to draw her into an explanation of what she had meant.

'Yes. A fortnight.'

'You took two weeks off last year in a stretch…' he reminded her.

'But I didn't leave the country.'

He had assumed she had. Of course when he had shown interest she had shrugged her shoulders and thrown him a something and nothing reply.

'Where did you go?' he asked curiously. 'I recall you took a fortnight off in October…not a brilliant time of year to relax in this country—not if you're looking for anything other than wall-to-wall rain and wind…'

'Last October the weather was beautiful.'

She tensed as he unwittingly came close to a subject she definitely had no intention of talking about. He might have dragged Oliver's name out of her, but that had been unavoidable. She should have had the foresight to know that her resignation would prompt his curiosity. Beyond that, however… No, there were no more roads she would be lured down.

'Was it?'

'Yes, it was. You must be keen to get off the phone, Leandro. Are you at home?'

'Not currently.'

Emily wondered where he was and assumed the obvious. Her voice was correspondingly cool when she said, after a brief hesitation, 'I'll make sure not to disturb you for the remainder of the evening, even if I need to ask you anything.'

'And why would that be?'

'I'm assuming that you're on one of your dates.'

She could have kicked herself. Yet again her tongue had run away from her and she needed to rescue this unruly twist in the conversation—one that had been prompted by *her*!

She wondered if the stress of everything happening in her life at the moment had weakened her defences. Whether, combined with that, the sudden, unexpected shift in her normal working relations with Leandro had further thrown her off course.

Kicking herself every time she slipped up wasn't going to help matters.

'In which case,' she added briskly, 'I wouldn't dream of interrupting.' She emitted a forced chuckle at this point, if only to demonstrate to him how fatuous she actually found their conversation. 'I do know that you don't like to be disturbed when you're with one of your…your…'

'My…? Don't forget you've made yourself crystal-clear on what you think of my…my… Now, how *would* you describe them…?'

'I never said anything about the sort of women you go out with,' Emily muttered. 'I only told you that I don't like running errands involving them on your behalf. I've only met a couple of them and they both seemed very…very… nice…'

'Damned with faint praise.'

'Oh, this is ridiculous!' Emily burst out angrily. 'I don't want to be having this conversation with you. If you're out with someone then I'll make sure you're not disturbed. If you need to get in touch with me tomorrow for some reason then you have my mobile number. I shall make sure I check it at regular intervals just in case.'

Leandro, who had no time for any show of histrionics in women, relaxed and half closed his eyes. This was the most rattled he had ever heard her. In fact over the past twenty-four hours she had blossomed into a real three-dimensional person, and he was enjoying the conversation—passing histrionics and all.

'And you'll be in London should I need to call on you to come in for some reason? Highly unlikely but, as you pointed out, a fortnight with both of us out of the office is unheard of…'

'No,' Emily said shortly. 'I probably won't be in London if I have a day off. Would you like me to come in to work after all?'

'No…'

Leandro found his mind wandering off course as his imagination, previously rusty, kicked into gear. A day off having mind-blowing sex with the mystery fiancé?

'I think I'll cope. You go off and do…whatever it is you have planned. Excluding, of course, that terminally boring retail therapy which you're not into. I'll see you at the airport. Bring your computer, Emily. And don't forget… pack for the weather…'

CHAPTER THREE

EMILY ARRIVED AT the airport with time to kill. She had had a sleepless night. Various random scenarios of what lay ahead of her for the next two weeks had ensured a disturbed sleep and now, with the bustle of people around her pulling cases, peering around for check-in desks, browsing in the shops and buying stacks of magazines and confectionery, she anxiously glanced around for Leandro.

He had instructed her on where to meet him. Whilst every other check-in desk was fronted by long queues, the first-class check-in for their flight was calm and empty. She could see people glancing at her with envy and kept her eyes firmly pinned in front of her.

She had packed economically and sparingly and kept her wardrobe as neutral as possible for a fortnight in the sun. Nothing flowery or girlish. Nothing to suggest that she was there for any other reason aside from business. Her single one-piece swimsuit was black. She had no intention of frolicking in a pool in a bikini. Or even stepping foot in one if she could help it.

Leandro's dark, deep voice behind her made her jump; she swung round to find him far too close to her for her liking, and automatically took a step back.

'I hope you haven't been waiting too long.' His voice was amused as he gave her the once-over.

Her fair hair was neatly in place, pulled back from her face and twisted into her style of choice, which was a bun designed to demonstrate that its wearer was anything but frivolous. She had traded in the more severe grey suit in favour of something a little less formal but still, in the end, a suit. Cream jacket with sleeves to the elbow, navy blue tee shirt underneath, cream skirt and a pair of flat shoes. Her entire outfit shrieked *business*, and if he hadn't had a tantalising glimpse behind the stern façade, he could have been forgiven for thinking that the woman looking up at him was completely devoid of personality.

But, oh, she wasn't. Never had been. Even though she had tried her hardest to camouflage that fact. And now...

'Can't stand airport waiting...'

He held out his hand for her passport and Emily stood back while he handled the check-in. Did he notice how the young girl behind the desk had gone bright red and was stumbling over her little speech about the first-class lounge and where they could find it? Or, as a practised charmer who worked his way through glamorous women the way a gourmand worked his way through a Michelin-starred meal, was he casually immune to the attention he commanded from the opposite sex?

Her lips thinned and she turned away.

'Which is why,' he continued, striding off as she fell in step with him, 'I tend to get to airports as late as possible. Tell me how your day was yesterday? What did you do?'

'I...I...had a few things to put into place...'

Leandro looked down at her. In flats she reached slightly above his shoulder and it made a change from the women he dated, who were all much shorter than he was.

'You've brought your computer, I take it?'

Emily exhaled a sigh of relief that he wasn't going to pin her down into trying to avoid yet another inroad into her private life. 'Of course I did.' She launched into a discussion on some of the deals he was currently working on and ignored his patent lack of animated response. 'Did anything urgent crop up yesterday?' she asked, if only to ensure their conversation remained on neutral ground.

He turned to look at her.

'Are you really interested?'

They had both stopped and the crowds parted around them. For a second her breath caught painfully in her throat and, having made a concerted effort not to look at him— *really* look at him—she now discovered that she couldn't peel her eyes away.

Next to him, she knew she looked stiff, awkwardly dressed in her lightweight suit which was hardly suitable for long-haul travel but which felt so much safer than a pair of comfortable trousers and a casual tee shirt. He looked cool, sophisticated, expensive. He was wearing a pair of black jeans and a polo shirt with a discreet logo on the front. No jacket. Loafers. His pull-along case was a small black leather affair, with no glaringly obvious outward evidence of having cost a lot, but it was easy to tell at a glance that it did.

Her mouth went dry as he continued to stare at her with those dark, dark eyes which had never before seemed to impact on her senses the way they were doing now.

'Of course I am. Why wouldn't I be? I've been working on some of those…um…deals for weeks…months…'

Leandro broke the connection and began walking again towards Immigration, where they were waved through, and directly to the first-class lounge, where once again they were treated to the very highest levels of respect and fawning.

She would have said that money talked, but she knew that he would have commanded the same attention if he

had been broke. There was just something about the man
that seemed to make people automatically obey.

'And yet you won't be seeing the conclusion of most of
them. So why bother to feign interest?'

'Just because I'll be…leaving…it doesn't mean that I'm
not one hundred per cent committed to doing my utmost
to…to…make sure the work gets done on them.' She found
herself sitting on a plush sofa and a waiter appeared from
thin air to take orders for drinks or food—presumably
whatever they wanted.

Leandro shrugged. 'In that case why don't you call up
the Edinburgh file on your computer and we can go through
it.'

He gave her the most polite of looks and Emily struggled
to manufacture a smile in return.

He was bored. He obviously thought that mentally she
had already defected, and he could barely summon up an
interest in discussing work with her. It made sense. The
only reason she was tagging along on this jaunt was because
he wanted to keep an eye on her and make sure she didn't
get up to Heaven knew what. Treason? The illegal sale of
company secrets to 'the other side'? Didn't he know her *at
all* after nearly two years of working with her?

No. He didn't. He didn't know a thing about her. And,
if she could spring an engagement on him, a fiancé lurking in the wings, then he must wonder what other surprises
she might have in store?

With less than her usual aplomb she dutifully brought
up the file and was keenly aware of him shifting his big
body towards her so that they could browse through the
information together.

She went through all the motions. After a lifetime of
holding her emotions in check there was no tremor to her
voice, nothing at all to betray her crazy jumpiness. She

could feel his eyes moving from the screen to her profile and wanted to scream at him at least to do her the favour of fully concentrating—because if he didn't then her nerves would fray just a little more at the edges.

'Have you any idea how hot it will be when we land at the airport?' he asked, when she had finished a long-winded spiel on the various obstacles that had been put in the way of the deal completion, and Emily grimaced.

'I didn't think we were discussing the weather,' she said, which teetered precariously on the edge of being lippy—not that it mattered, considering she was practically no longer his employee and in no need of a reference.

'Is the rest of your wardrobe along the lines of what you're wearing now?'

Emily edged away from him and snapped shut her computer, turning to return it neatly to the smart case she had brought with her.

Why did she feel like a fool?

For no reason she was suddenly overwhelmed by an image of herself as a woman in her twenties, buttoned up and careful, always on her guard. She could barely remember a time when she hadn't been that way. The last boyfriend she had had—a brief six-month fling four years previously—had been an unmitigated disaster. Her inexperience had been agonising and her inherently suspicious nature had gradually seeped into the relationship, suffocating it, until they'd parted company amidst a welter of embarrassing platitudes about keeping in touch and remaining friends. They never had.

Then she thought of the women Leandro dated: sexy, full-on women, who weren't cocooned in a veritable fortress of self-protective defence mechanisms that would have rivalled any Victorian maiden's chastity belt.

What must he think of her?

She told herself that it hardly mattered, and yet her tight mouth, silenced on everything that was in the slightest bit personal, now seemed ludicrous and childish.

Emily drove aside that disturbing vision of herself and cleared her throat.

'I…I naturally want to dress in a suitably…er…'

'Restrained manner for an eight-hour flight to the Caribbean?'

'I wouldn't have felt comfortable in jeans and a tee shirt,' she said flatly.

A tide of colour washed up her face and she had to bite back the nervous temptation to jump into a qualifying speech when he remained looking at her in silence.

'And you feel comfortable in a starchy linen suit?'

'It's practical.'

'If you say so.'

He pulled out his top-of-the-range sleek tablet and flicked it on.

Emily interpreted that as a signal that their conversation was over. She had brought her book with her, a lightweight crime thriller, but would he launch into a sarcastic aside about her choice of reading matter if she fished it out of her handbag? So instead she extracted some material she had printed off the last day she had been at work—background reading on the holiday compound to which they were headed—and buried herself in it.

Leandro, working his way through a series of emails from his family to which he owed replies, glanced across to where her lowered head and stiff body language were visible signs of her armour.

What *was* it about this woman? And why was he suddenly so obsessed with finding out what made her tick? He wasn't taking her to the Caribbean to remove her from possible secret-sharing with competitors. She would never do any such thing and he knew that. No. He was taking her with him because…he wanted time with her. Time in which he could indulge his sudden curiosity. Or maybe it irked him that she could just walk out on him when he needed her? Since when did women walk out on him? Even though it might be on a professional basis…

One thing was for sure: it was going to be a hellishly long flight if they both maintained the tight-lipped silence she seemed to want.

Attuned to her on a level that was frankly irritating, he boarded the plane, settled into his seat—a comfortable recliner that could convert into a full bed at the press of a button—and he noted with some amusement that even when all the lights had been switched off and they could do as they pleased she remained upright, reading a book which she had ferreted out of her bag.

He reclined his seat, switched off the little reading light, debated whether to rescue her from her obvious discomfort by introducing a little light work-related banter and then decided against it.

How, Emily thought crossly, could the man just *fall asleep*? On a plane?

He was way too long for his seat, even when it was fully down, converted into a bed. She stole a sidelong glance at his averted profile. There was something vulnerable about a person when he was asleep. The lines that gave his face definition were smoothed out into peaceful tranquillity and she found herself mesmerised by the way he looked.

He was no longer the hard-edged boss who'd so recently been threatening her with the force of his personality and the animal magnetism of his physical presence. There was a boyish handsomeness to his face that made something inside her squirm.

She returned to her book, but found herself glancing

across again and again to him, her eyes lingering on his face, then drifting down the length of his body to the broadness of his chest, the strength in his hands which were lightly clasped on his stomach, the muscular length of his legs…

She gulped and looked away quickly, her heart thumping inside her, as she took in the obvious bulge of his crotch.

What on earth was happening to her?

If she had been really and truly engaged, anticipating marriage to the man of her dreams, then she knew that her thoughts would not be striking off at a tangent now—that she would be able to look at Leandro and not feel this unaccustomed rush of forbidden attraction. But she *wasn't* really and truly engaged, was she?

Abruptly she turned away and thought about Oliver—the guy her boss thought she was crazy about…the guy who should have been jealous and possessive of her. What a joke. Yes, she would be marrying him, but her reasons were all cynically practical.

She needed the money and he would be her passport to that.

She must have drifted into a sleep of sorts, and to feel herself being shaken awake was so disorientating that she gave a little yelp of alarm and jerked forward. It took her a few seconds to register where she was. Not in her bed but on the plane, her seat still fully upright. Her heart was going like a jackhammer inside her and she could taste the remnants of her dream as it was chased away by Leandro's hand on her shoulder, shaking her.

Her immediate instinct to pull away fought against the lethargy of being abruptly awakened and she stared at him.

'What are you doing?' She had left her linen jacket on and it had rucked up. Through the stiff fabric his hand was warm and heavy, burning a direct path to her shoulder. It acted like an anchor, weighing her down so that she felt she couldn't move.

'What the hell were you dreaming about?'

'What?'

His face was so close to hers that she could feel his warm breath fanning her cheek. His hair was tousled and he looked achingly, sinfully sexy, all rumpled and bed-room-eyed.

'Dreaming,' Leandro repeated, his hand moving from her shoulder to absently caress her neck and jawline. 'You were dreaming, Emily.'

'I woke you up. I'm sorry.'

She could scarcely breathe. She was hyper-conscious of his hand on her face. She was certain that he barely realised what he was doing, but *she* was all too aware of it, and yet she found that she couldn't budge an inch, couldn't retreat to the safety of her own side of the seat.

'Don't worry about me,' he cut in impatiently.

His eyes roved over her flushed face and lighted on her parted mouth. Immediately and without warning he felt the pain of sudden arousal. Her cheeks were pink, her hair was struggling free of its constraints and appeared to be longer than he had imagined, and her wide blue eyes were hazy with the remnants of confusion. She looked every bit the young girl she was—the girl she tried so hard to conceal beneath an icy, untouchable veneer.

A wayward thought insinuated itself into his head. She looked *sexy*. Sexy and, with those parted lips, eminently kissable.

'What were you dreaming about?'

'Nothing.' Emily drew back and he removed his hand from her shoulder. She felt its absence in a way that disturbed her, but she kept her gaze as steady as she could on his face.

Yes, she had been dreaming, and the dream came back to her now in jagged bits and pieces. Oliver. Actually marrying him. What that would entail. A nasty dream of dark shadows and fear. And wrapped up inside the dream had been Leandro—although now, awake, she couldn't remember what exactly he had been doing there.

'Quite an extreme reaction for a dream about nothing.'

'Did I…mention anyone…?'

Leandro stared down into her blue eyes and wondered what accounted for that wary look.

'No,' he admitted. 'But you yelped as though you were scared.'

'I've never been a quiet sleeper,' Emily said truthfully, if only to explain herself.

'No?'

She hesitated and threw him a reluctant smile which he found unreasonably captivating—perhaps because it was such a rare occurrence.

'I went through a period of sleepwalking when I was… younger…when I was in my early teens. Ever since then I've been a jumpy sleeper.'

Leandro imagined her as a young teenager and immediately wanted to know more about her, wanted her to open up to him before she released the shutters and returned to hide behind them.

'That must have driven your siblings mad,' he murmured encouragingly.

'I don't have any siblings. I'm an only child.' No big secret there, and yet it felt like a confidence of huge proportions.

'So this marriage must be a big deal for your parents…?'

'I…'

Leandro continued to lock her with his dark eyes, making retreat from the conversation difficult.

'It's just me and my mum.' Emily's mouth tightened. As soul-baring went, this was as far as it was going to go—she was amazed that she had actually got to this point in the first place.

Leandro waited and then into the deepening silence said lightly, 'Peace and quiet...'

'What do you mean?'

'I mean, as an only boy with four sisters, peace and quiet was never something I could bank on from one day to the next.'

'Four sisters...?' Emily grinned and stole a glance at him. When he raised his eyebrows and smiled at her she felt her pulse quicken and her skin prickle. Aeroplane chatter, she thought a little nervously. No harm done.

'Four sisters—and they all liked experimenting with their make-up on me...'

Emily burst out laughing and Leandro thought that she didn't do nearly enough of that. He wondered whether her fiancé brought out that side of her—the side that would spontaneously laugh, would make her shed the look of someone carrying the weight of the world on her shoulders... And he felt a spurt of irritation towards the man...

'I don't believe you!'

'Believe it.' He grinned with wry amusement. 'Clearly I was only four or five at the time, but I still bear the scars.'

'And you didn't develop a taste for wearing make-up in later life?'

Leandro burst out laughing. 'So far I can happily avoid cosmetic counters...'

'Then the scars can't have been so ingrained.'

Their eyes tangled as they both shared the same moment of relaxed banter and for a few seconds Emily's heart seemed to skip a beat—several beats. Her mouth went dry and there was a strange roaring in her ears.

'Have you…? Have you…?'

'Have I what?'

'Have you…got any idea as to whether there are any last-minute things that might need doing at the hotel when we arrive…?'

She barely recognised the breathlessness in her voice, but at least she had managed to drag the conversation back down to Planet Earth—although when he lowered his eyes and moved fractionally further back she felt herself missing that moment of warmth that had suddenly and unexpectedly ignited between them.

Leandro wondered if she might just scrabble in her multi-purpose handbag and extract her laptop computer so that she could hide behind it.

'I've appointed some good people to oversee all the building work. Everything should be in pristine condition when we arrive. Bar cutting a ribbon, the place should be up and running and ready for its first happy holidaymakers to arrive.'

'Its first extremely wealthy holidaymakers…'

'Are you telling me that you disapprove of people who have sufficient money enjoying expensive holidays abroad?'

'Not at all.'

But bitterness had found its way into her voice. There had been a time, when she was growing up, when she had been on those sorts of holidays. She could barely remember them—she had made great strides in blanking those memories out of her head—but right now they crept back in. Those holidays as a child, when she and her parents had gone to expensive hotels in expensive destinations.

'No, of course I don't,' she said in a more normal voice. 'After all, if your hotel is fully booked then it provides countless jobs for the locals, and I know from reading the literature that it's all going to be eco-friendly. The food will be locally sourced…everything's been cleverly done to cause as little disturbance as possible to the natural environment…'

'You're beginning to sound like a tour guide,' Leandro said drily.

He realised that he would miss this about her—her ability to absorb the bigger picture of any deal he undertook, to transform it into much more than a money-making exercise.

What was she thinking…handing in that letter of resignation?

He raked his fingers through his hair in frustration and shifted in his seat. However much he paid, there was a limit to how much space was available on an aircraft, and right now he wanted to walk about, flex his muscles—do something highly physical to counterbalance the restlessness inside him at the thought of her dumping him.

No, he amended mentally, she wasn't *dumping him*. She was moving on to greener pastures.

It was a notion that didn't make him feel any better. Greener pastures with some guy she could barely bring herself to mention! Was there something wrong with the man? He felt there probably was or she would have pulled out a wallet full of photos by now, however tight-lipped she was by nature.

'Perhaps that might be my next job,' Emily quipped without thinking.

'So you *will* be getting another job after you're hitched to this man of yours…?'

He wondered where the time had gone. They would be landing in under an hour and he felt as though he could have carried on talking to her for another eight.

'Possibly,' Emily murmured vaguely. 'Gosh. Is that the

time? I must go to the ladies'…freshen up… I can't believe the time's gone so quickly! Literally *flown past*…!'

Leandro scowled and watched as she slipped out of the seat. Keen eyes followed her hands as she smoothed the prissy shirt and readjusted the equally prissy jacket. She was as slender as a reed and he wondered if she worked out.

He turned to gaze out of the window, down at the bank of clouds. He was finding it hard to get his mind off the woman. Usually on long-haul flights he could devote his time to work. Huge amounts could be achieved with the luxury of not being interrupted. He glanced down at his laptop and realised that he had barely skimmed the surface of what he had optimistically intended to do.

He was in the act of snapping shut the laptop when he looked up and saw her returning from the bathroom.

For a few seconds, he was deprived of the power of coherent thought. She had brushed back her hair and done away with the sensible bun. Instead she had swept it into a low ponytail which hung over one shoulder like a gold, silky rope. Her hair was long. Much longer than he had imagined. She had also done away with the jacket, and her clinging tee shirt, while still the height of modesty, was sufficiently tight to show off the shape of her high, small breasts.

Emily didn't want to look at him as she walked back to her seat. She felt conspicuous and she wasn't entirely sure why, because her outfit was hardly revealing.

'Your turn.' She addressed the armrest. 'It's now or never.'

Leandro was grappling to find something to say. For the first time in his life he was lost for words as he mumbled something before sliding past her.

The plane landed and the passengers were disgorged into an early evening which was still sticky and warm.

'We need an interconnecting flight to the island,' he said to her. 'I have a private island hopper on standby.'

He fought an insane urge to release her hair *just to see what it looked like loose.* It joined the host of other inappropriate thoughts that had recently afflicted him and he cursed himself yet again for looking at a woman who was taken by someone else. There were plenty of fish in the sea, he had always thought, for him not to be bothered with trying to catch one that belonged to someone else.

But he wasn't *trying to catch her,* he reasoned firmly to himself as they cleared their bags and were ushered to the adjoining strip where their plane awaited them. He was simply trying to work her out—and if he happened, in passing, to notice how crazily attractive she was, then who could blame him? He was a one hundred per cent red-blooded male after all!

She moved with a calm, unhurried grace that didn't try to draw attention to itself. In the closed confines of an office it was something he had never really noticed before, but it was evident now, when she was surrounded by open space.

He was aware of her asking questions about their flight to the island and joking nervously about the reliability of such a small plane, which looked barely big enough to hold a handful of people, and he was aware that he was responding in a perfectly natural manner. All the time his rebellious mind was on a rollercoaster ride.

What would she look like without those clothes on? With that long vanilla-blonde hair spread across a pillow and that half-smile of hers inviting him to take her? Her body would be smooth and supple and pale, her breasts small and shapely, with rosebud nipples... He wondered what they would taste like. The thought of filling his mouth with one of them brought him back down to earth with an agonising bump just as they boarded the light plane.

'I've never travelled like this before.'

Leandro looked at her. Already, outside, darkness had descended abruptly, and the violet colours that had streaked the sky had faded into deep velvet blackness. As the little plane taxied down the runway and took off like a small, buzzing mosquito they could have been anywhere in the world. Anywhere hot. The temperature was in the eighties and Emily's face was shiny with perspiration.

'In a small, dangerous object hardly bigger than a washing machine and with the engine of an underpowered lawnmower?'

'Please don't say that.'

Leandro laughed with genuine amusement. 'Don't worry. This plane wouldn't dare drop out of the sky with *me* on board.'

Emily relaxed. His voice was light and teasing and she felt some of her nerves about the short flight begin to ebb away. 'I had no idea you had such power over inanimate objects,' she returned in similar vein, because it distracted her from a worst-case scenario that involved them all plummeting to the ground in a disarray of twisted metal.

'Reassuring, wouldn't you agree? I know the pilot personally. He's excellent.'

'Have you ever been in something as small as this before?'

'I can go one step better. I've flown something not dissimilar...'

'You haven't?' She found she was totally absorbed by what he was saying. His lazy, teasing gaze held her spellbound.

'When I was sixteen.'

'I don't believe you.'

Leandro chuckled and threw her a superior look that was strangely boyish. 'Flew over my father's ranch in a light aircraft which he kept securely housed out of reach of curious juvenile hands—or so he fondly imagined.'

'You *stole* your father's plane?' She grappled with the twin notions of living on a ranch which housed its own personal light aeroplane and Leandro as a teenager, breaking and entering to get his hands on it.

On the back burner were all her fears about being on such a tiny plane, about having to spend a fortnight in his company, about what lay ahead of her beyond that…

'I hijacked it for an hour and a half…'

'Your parents must have been worried to death. How dangerous!' But hadn't she always known that he had that devil-may-care side to him? It was part of what made him such a formidable opponent in the business arena.

'Not dangerous,' Leandro murmured in a low drawl that sent shivers rippling up and down her spine, 'just challenging. And if I know anything about myself it's that I can never back away from a challenge…'

Why did she feel that the remark went beyond the remembered thrill of flying solo at the age of sixteen? Why did she feel such a shiver of fierce, dark *excitement*? It terrified her, and not for the first time since she had confessed to her engagement to Oliver she wished desperately that the man she was committed to marrying was more than just a means to a very necessary end. More than ever she wished that she could hold on to him as a barrier against the effect Leandro seemed to be having on her.

'But surely even if you'd flown with someone before you would have been scared…?' Her heart was thumping inside her and every nerve-ending in her body felt primed, on red-hot alert.

'Of course I wasn't scared,' Leandro said with a casual shrug and the same half-smile that made her feel so unsteady. 'I was a teenager. Since when do teenagers feel fear? And besides,' he admitted, 'I'd had a few flying lessons with one of the ranch hands. I only felt afraid when I landed the plane and spotted my parents waiting for me.'

He threw back his head and laughed.

God, it was heady having her attention focused so completely on him. It made him feel like the teenager he no longer was. He was quite accustomed to having women hanging on to his every word, but *this* woman…

'What did they say?'

'Grounded for life.' He grinned. 'Of course it was impossible for them to stick to that threat. Grounded for three days and then a course of flying lessons, so that if I ever felt inclined to take the plane up again they would at least know I would be able to fully handle the controls…a win-win situation, as it turned out…' He smiled fondly at the memory. 'We're going to be landing in a few minutes…'

Emily hadn't even noticed that the plane had been dipping lower, but now she broke free of his gaze to peer down into velvety darkness. She could just about make out twinkling of lights as they looped down. They hadn't removed their seat belts and she clutched the arm of her chair until her knuckles were white. Anyone would have imagined that she had never flown before, and of course she had. Many times when she had been younger. But never in something as tiny as this.

They bumped to a shuddering stop and then they were out in the warm Caribbean night, with the sounds of tropical insects all around them. It was a little disorientating. The island was small and there was none of the usual chaos of a proper airport.

She didn't resist when he cupped her elbow with his hand to guide her towards the little terminal, which was empty except for a few employees. Behind them their bags were being brought on a trolley. The sound of the soft, lilting accents around her was as foreign as the sounds of the insects and the fragrant warmth of the night.

This might be a horrendous work-related trip during which she would be closeted with a man who got to her whether she admitted it to herself or not, but she still felt the stirrings of excitement at being out of London, on exotically foreign soil.

Without looking at him, she reached to undo the ponytail and shook her hair free, before scooping it all up once again in a fluid gesture, back into a ponytail—a high one.

Against the darkness surrounding them and the smooth, deep mahogany skin of the airport workers who had surrounded them, and were laughing and chatting as they wheeled their bags through, her paleness was intensely eye-catching. He would go as far as to say *erotic*.

And from nowhere sprang the disturbing thought that this was not merely a challenge…this was danger.

CHAPTER FOUR

THE WOMAN WAS ENGAGED!

Over the next two days that was the only thing that acted as a brake on an imagination that was now firing on all cylinders. That brief moment of companionship on the island hopper—when she had let her guard down, when he had felt as though he was seeing yet another tantalising glimpse of the woman she really was under the mask—had disappeared.

Frustratingly, she had retreated behind her professional façade, and he had had no time to try and work his way beneath it because much of the time they were in the company of other people.

On the island he was nothing short of a minor celebrity. The locals loved him. He had been single-handedly responsible for creating a huge number of jobs. He paid very well. He had sent several of them on courses abroad. Everyone was looking forward to a boom in tourism, thanks to his innovative hotel. His influence had trickled its way into all sectors of the economy.

As soon as they'd arrived they'd been told the great news by the manager in charge of the project that a television crew from one of the major channels in America would be coming for a few days, to cover the opening of the hotel and analyse what it meant for the economy.

Emily felt as though she had entered a strange new world where she had suddenly been elevated to celebrity status purely because everyone seemed to think that she came as part of a package deal with Leandro.

They'd been wined and dined by the great and the good on the island. The local paper had snapped pictures of them. And in the ensuing hectic whirlwind of social activity she had thankfully been able to shakily put her working hat back on and keep it firmly in place.

Her swimsuit had remained at the back of a drawer, and if she had attended dinners and luncheons in attire that was a little over-formal for the surroundings, then at least she felt comfortable in her clothes, and she had firmly resisted the pleas of several of the local businessmen's wives to go shopping for more 'Caribbean-style stuff'. By which she had deduced they meant sarongs, flip-flops, transparent floaty dresses and other bits and pieces which she knew would have made her feel even more vulnerable than she already did.

Now, tonight, for the first time since they had arrived on the island, they would be dining alone in the hotel restaurant, sampling the standard of the cuisine. A selection of taster plates would be brought for them, along with suitable wines.

'Perhaps you and Antoine should do that on your own?' she had suggested the night before. 'I mean, he *is* the head chef. Wouldn't it be more appropriate if you had him there with you?'

'He'll be behind the scenes,' Leandro had pointed out, in a tone of voice that had suggested he knew very well that she was trying to avoid his company. 'Do you suggest he cooks, then quickly changes out of his chef clothes and scampers over to my table so that he can pretend that he's tasting his own food for the first time?'

Emily looked at her reflection in the mirror and felt a

shiver of nervous tension ripple through her. She had been given one of the luxury cabanas which sat nestled amidst palm trees and cleverly landscaped lawns that were bursting with colour. She had been told to evaluate it in as detached a manner as possible and get back to him with any suggestions for improvement.

There were none. The cabana was the last word in luxury, from the cool bamboo furniture to the sophisticated adjoining wet room. There was also a thoughtfully positioned full-length mirror, to accommodate women who wanted to make sure that they looked perfect when they stepped foot outside the cabana, and it was this mirror which now reflected back to her an image that was stunningly different from the one she had spent the past year and a half cultivating.

The sun had given her skin a pale gold hue and brought out a sprinkling of freckles across the bridge of her nose. Against the tan her eyes appeared bluer, her lashes thicker and her hair lighter.

Instead of the habitual bun, which she had continued to wear even out here, she had decided to leave her hair loose, and it fell over her shoulders and halfway down her back in a display of wild abandon. The heat and humidity had done something to it—brought out curls and waves she'd never known she had.

Returned to the wardrobe were her neat ensembles. She had brought out one of her two less formal dresses—a turquoise wraparound that showed off lots of leg and bare arms. It was nothing anyone could possibly consider *daring*, and yet as she did a half-twirl in front of the mirror she *felt* daring.

Leandro, having a drink in the bar, was only aware of Emily's entrance because the little group of men he was chatting to all fell silent. Drink in hand, he turned around slowly and for a few seconds his mind went completely blank. He took a fortifying gulp of rum and water and forced himself to smile and move towards her, murmuring a few words to the guys around him by way of taking his leave.

'The television crew will be arriving tomorrow,' he said, dragging his eyes away from her with difficulty. 'Lots of promotional shots which will benefit us and benefit the community here at large.'

Emily smiled politely. He hadn't said a word about how she looked, and although she hadn't dressed for him it would have only been courteous to pay her some sort of compliment, wouldn't it?

'That's brilliant!'

'And, if you look to your left, you'll see that they've specifically laid a table for us. It's a demo of how all the tables will be laid when the place is full. I've told my people here that there must be no shortage of attention to detail. Feel free to comment on the job they've done...'

'Of course.'

She was so conscious of him next to her that she felt faint. Something about being there, seeing him in different surroundings...

She might be at great pains to stick to formalities, but he was not. His clothes were cool and casual. No suit, no tie, no restrictive jacket. Now he was in a pair of light-coloured Bermuda shorts, a black polo shirt and loafers without socks. And a couple of days in the blazing sun had lent his complexion an even more burnished hue.

Could the man look any sexier? She had to feebly remind herself that this was just the sort of package that gave him a sense of entitlement to women—the sort of casual sense of entitlement that repelled her.

'But I'm sure it'll all be perfect—just as the room is perfect.'

'That's the difference between a good hotel and a really great one. A great one takes nothing for granted and never gets complacent.'

Had he been complacent about *her*? Was that why she had handed in her resignation? However little need there might be for her to hold down a job, surely an intelligent woman like her would still want the distraction of work that provided a challenge? Unless, of course...

'Are you pregnant?' he asked abruptly as they sat at the table opposite one another.

It took a few seconds for the softly worded question to sink in. Emily had been absently admiring the surroundings. The eating area was fashioned along the lines of an enormous gazebo. It was covered, so that diners would be protected from the elements, but open at the sides so that there was an unimpeded view of the sea, now just a dark body of water lapping gently along the shore. Bird-feeders had been strategically placed on the outside so that during the day there were always birds dipping down to feed and filling the air with their chorus. It was idyllic.

'I beg your pardon?'

'It never occurred to me, but it makes sense. The rushed marriage, the resignation letter... Are you pregnant? Because if you are then I have no problem keeping the job open for you until you feel fit to return to work...'

He pushed his chair back and angled it to one side, so that he could cross his legs while he kept his eyes firmly pinned to her face. In the mellow pool of light her face was soft and flushed...

There was an expression on it that he couldn't put his finger on until she said, with biting cynicism, 'I'm anything *but* pregnant. Kids?' She laughed and took a long gulp of the wine that had been brought over to them. 'That will *never* be on my agenda.'

As hooks went, this one was irresistible. Leandro had never experienced such intense curiosity about a woman. On every level he wanted to know more, even though he recognised the weakness behind the pull on his senses.

'I thought it was the dream of most women to have children…' he murmured encouragingly. 'Diamond rock on the finger, walk up the aisle, the pitter-patter of tiny feet…'

'Not me.' Emily took another energy-boosting sip of wine and realised that her glass was empty. It was quickly refilled. Part of the excellent service.

'And does the lucky guy in your life know that?'

'What lucky guy in my life?' She was momentarily bewildered. 'Oh. Oliver.' She shrugged. 'Absolutely.'

'You seem very young to have made such a momentous decision…or perhaps your fiancé is behind it? Is he divorced? Maybe with a family of his own already? Sometimes middle-aged men with grown children don't want to add to the tally when they decide to marry someone much younger than them…'

Emily recognised fishing when she heard it, and although she should have terminated the meandering conversation the wine had dulled her senses. She wasn't accustomed to alcohol. She could feel herself wavering on the brink of saying more than she would ever have dreamt of saying had she been her usual careful, alert self.

It was so strange, being here with him. In the warm, shadowy night he was no longer her boss, no longer the man she privately scorned, no longer someone in whom she should never confide. The boundaries between them were blurred, and his deep, lazy voice was oddly enticing.

'I didn't think we were here to talk about me,' she said, in a voice that lacked its usual firm conviction.

Leandro sipped his wine and allowed the conversation to drop as they consulted their menus. He chatted briefly about the offerings for dinner. Her soft hair fell in waves around her face and he was mesmerised as she tucked a few strands behind her ear and chewed her lip thoughtfully at the menu.

Perhaps there should be more fish, she thought aloud. After all, they *were* in the Caribbean, and wouldn't guests expect more than just a couple of fishy options?

'I take it you like fish…?'

'Love it. Especially as I don't often cook it at home.'

Leandro wondered what her home was like. A reflection of her complex personality? Sharp modern designs? Abstract reproductions hanging on the walls?

'I don't often cook,' he said by way of an amused rejoinder, and Emily tilted her head to one side and looked at him.

'You know what? That doesn't surprise me.'

'No? And why is that?'

'Because men like you don't.'

Leandro stilled. He looked at her narrowly and she met his eyes without blinking.

'Men like me?' he said coolly. 'Are we going to revisit the tired topic of the way you think I use women?'

He sat back as their starters were set in front of them and plates neatly adjusted to the perfect position. Their glasses were refilled but then they were left alone, which was good. Her attention had drifted down to her starter, but Leandro thought that if she figured she could now change the conversation and start talking about the table service, or some such other bland topic, then she would have to think again.

'You have lots of money,' she mumbled, picking at her starter and then digging in with more enthusiasm because it was delicious—a cool salad of leaves and fresh mango with spicy prawns piled on top. 'Why would you cook for yourself when you can pay someone else to do it for you?'

'Because I may actually *like* cooking but lack the time to put into it.'

'Do you?'

'Do I what?'

'Really like cooking but just don't have the time to do it...?'

'Not exactly...' Leandro shot her a sexy grin that made her breath catch in her throat and brought a reluctant smile to her lips. 'I *have* produced the occasional success-ful omelette, but I'm no expert in the kitchen. Well...' He shrugged his broad shoulders in a gesture that was typi-cally *his*. 'Growing up with a horde of sisters *does* have its advantages...'

'Aside from plying you with make-up when you were young, they spoiled you? Is that what you're saying?'

She thought wistfully of when she was a kid, always wishing for a sibling... Now, more than ever, it would have been nice to have someone with whom she could share all her worries. Her destiny would still not have been the big happy family scenario, but at least she wouldn't have been on her own coping with all her problems.

'An only boy...' He tilted his head and looked at her with a half-smile. 'What can you expect?'

He was momentarily distracted by the removal of plates and kept his curiosity at bay as she chatted about the food, made all the right noises about its quality. He refilled her glass and called for another bottle of wine to be brought to them. Only when their main courses were set in front of them did he return to the subject that had been on his mind.

'So,' he drawled, 'you were telling me about the fiancé with the family...'

Emily blinked. 'I have no idea what you're talking about.'

'You don't want kids because he already has a few of his own…?'

'Of course he doesn't have any kids!' She wondered how it was that her wineglass seemed to be permanently full. When she tried to marshal her thoughts they swirled away, just out of reach. She tried to grasp hold of an image of Oliver. 'He's the same age as me!'

'So neither of you is interested in prolonging the family line…'

'Do *you* intend to have kids? Get married? Settle down?'

She couldn't picture it. No, he was the sort of guy who would never settle down, and if he ever did then he would carry on leading the bachelor life. There were men like that. Handsome, charming, wealthy men, who just took what they wanted and didn't care about the people they hurt in the process.

Maudlin tears of self-pity tried to push their way to her eyes and she looked down hurriedly at her plate. Mysteriously, she had managed to finish most of the food that had been put in front of her, although she couldn't remember taking a single mouthful.

'Of course.'

Leandro pushed his plate to one side and sat forward. It was dark in the restaurant, with only the light from hanging lanterns and from the moon illuminating the tables. But he thought her voice sounded suspiciously unsteady, and the way she was staring down at her plate…

'Are you…'

'I'm fine,' she said abruptly. 'I don't usually have this much to drink. You were telling me about your plans to have a wife and children… I apologise. It's none of my business.'

Her head felt thick and cloudy. The sounds of the insects were clearer at night, and along with the warm, slight breeze and the magical, lazy lapping of the sea on the sandy beach they acted as a soporific drug, lulling her into puzzling territory. Part of her knew that they should not be talking like this, shouldn't be breaking down the barriers between them, but it just felt inevitable at that moment.

'I should tell you that I think the meal was wonderful…' She fought to drag the conversation back into familiar terrain. 'How did you manage to get hold of Antoine? He's a real find…'

'You're changing the subject.'

'Because this is about work, Leandro. This isn't a…a holiday… This isn't about two people getting to know one another. I'm here because I had no choice and…and…' She felt woozy. 'I think I'd like some coffee…'

'Of course.'

He ordered them both coffee before seamlessly continuing the conversation.

'And why shouldn't we make an attempt to get to know one another? Believe me, I'm the last person in the world to ever condone working relationships straying beyond sensible, acceptable boundaries, but making harmless small talk over a meal doesn't constitute that. So you have a fiancé. Why the secrecy? Do you think that by talking about him you're somehow going to cross enemy lines? You can't say that you'll be jeopardising your job or your references because you've handed in your resignation…'

He raked his fingers through his hair and wished she would stop looking at him with those huge, blue, dreamy eyes. She'd had a little too much to drink and the effect of the alcohol had been to soften her expression. She was leaning towards him, elbow on the table, chin propped in the cup of her hand. The blue dress—some sort of complicated wraparound affair—looked as though it was hanging onto its shape by the skin of its teeth. A couple of tugs and it would unwrap itself and drop to the ground in a pool of slippery fabric. His fingers itched to do just that—tug her free of it.

Her damned fiancé would have had a heart attack—*several* heart attacks—if he had been able to decipher the thoughts Leandro was having about his beloved girlfriend.

'And, to answer your question about my intention to have a family of my own one day...'

He was irritated to find himself spurred into speech. It definitely wasn't his usual style. And certainly not on a subject he had always been at great pains to avoid discussing with the opposite sex. Experience had taught him that leading questions about his long-term plans when it came to commitment usually ended badly.

But her attention was rapt, short-circuiting his common sense.

'Yes?'

Leandro shook his head and stared out for a few seconds at the open water. The beach was semi-lit and the black surface of the sea was streaked silver from the light. In accordance with his strict instructions, staff were keeping themselves at a distance.

'When the time is right and I meet the right woman,' he said gruffly, 'I won't hesitate to tie the knot.'

'Meet the right woman...?' Emily emitted a low, mirthless laugh. 'I never took you for the romantic sort...'

'No, I know exactly the sort you took me for. You made that crystal-clear.'

'Are you angry with me for telling you what I thought?'

'Surprised. Too surprised to be angry. And yet you never stopped to consider that I might have been one hundred per cent transparent in my dealings with women...'

'What do you mean?' Emily shot him a perplexed frown.

This dangerous conversation was thrilling. Every muscle and tendon in her body felt stretched to breaking point. She didn't want to carry on talking about this, delving into areas that should have been kept separate, and yet she just couldn't seem to resist. She was literally holding her breath and hanging on to his every word.

'I never led any of them on.'

He fixed his dark eyes on her face and thought he might have liked to let them linger there—but staring had its limits, and since when was he the kind of guy who *stared*?

'I never made promises I didn't feel I could keep. They knew what they were getting into from day one and I treated them like queens.'

'And yet none of them was your special soulmate…'

'You've got to kiss a lot of frogs… Is that what you did, Emily? Before you chanced upon Mr Right?'

'I haven't been on a worldwide search for a soulmate.'

Leandro looked at her, head inclined. Someone hovered, waiting to ask them how their meals had been, and he waved them aside without taking his eyes off her face. 'Does that mean that your fiancé has fitted the bill before you've even had a chance to explore all possible options?' he asked softly.

'I suppose you could say so,' Emily muttered.

She wiped her mouth and sat back, shakily aware of how close she had come to baring her soul to him.

'And now, if you don't mind, I'm a little tired.' She backed that up with a delicate forced yawn. 'So I think I'll retire to bed. Perhaps you could tell me what our plans are for tomorrow? Meetings? I know the TV crew are coming, so I expect you'll want to do…er…stuff in preparation…'

'What sort of stuff?'

'I don't know!' Emily snapped. 'Stuff. Make sure the

photos are taken from the right angles! I don't know anything about how the media circus works in a case like this!'

'Hardly a media circus. Some poor sod has landed the job of reporting on a fairly frivolous development on a tropical island. It's not going to make headlines across the world. And, in answer to your question, I'll let my PR team handle it. It'll be their first big tourist push and it'll be interesting to see how they cope. So tomorrow…why don't you take a little time out? We can have a look around the island.'

'Time—time out?' Emily stammered.

'It's the weekend. Even I am not such a slave-driver that I would insist you work weekends…'

He summoned Antoine and whilst he chatted with him, complimenting him on the meal and asking detailed questions about various culinary options for picky tourists, Emily took time out to digest what he had said. A day of sightseeing. Just the two of them? He certainly hadn't hinted at a convenient entourage of any kind.

Her mind was in a mild state of panic as she rose to her feet, to find that the effects of a little too much wine were far more pronounced now that she wasn't sitting down.

With difficulty, she took small, concentrated steps alongside him as they made their way out of the restaurant to their respective cabins, and as luck would have it a sudden attack of dizziness in combination with a lack of familiarity with her surroundings worked in perfect unison to send her flying over a dip in the ground.

She had a few panicked seconds during which she attempted to steady herself, and then she was on the soft ground, blood gushing from her foot where it had scraped against a protruding stone.

She didn't know which was worse. The stinging of her foot or the humiliation of being helped to her feet by Leandro and then, even more embarrassingly, finding her-

self swept up into his arms and carried to her cabana like
a sack of potatoes.

'Don't struggle.' He anticipated the protest she was about
to make. 'How the hell did *that* happen? No, don't bother.
You've had too much to drink.'

She might be tall but she was light. Her slender arms
looped around his neck, and the soft feel of her body
pressed against his made him grit his teeth together, because his body was again responding in ways that disre-
garded the constraints imposed by his head.

'I'm fine to walk,' Emily muttered half-heartedly.

'Your foot is pouring blood.'

'That's an exaggeration.'

'I'll sort it out.'

'Surely there must be a first aid…um…person on site?'

'Not in place yet…'

Was that strictly true? Leandro was pretty sure that he
could get all the medical help required at the snap of a finger—but, hell…what was the point for a little cut on a foot?
Nothing he couldn't handle. He'd never been queasy when
it came to blood. In fact, he had once debated whether to
go down the medical route but had decided against it. He
positively *liked* a bit of blood!

'Many staff will fall into place once the hotel is fully
operational. At the moment only essential members of the
team are here…'

They had reached her cabana, which was unlocked, and
he nudged the door open. For a few seconds the space was
disorientating in its darkness, then he found the light switch
and somehow managed to turn on the overhead light without putting her down.

The cabana was split into a large bedroom with an en-
suite bathroom, an outer room which functioned as a sitting
room, with comfortable chairs, a table, a television and a

bamboo desk on which, he noted, she had placed her computer, and a compact kitchen area with basic facilities for making tea and coffee. There was also a fridge, which was restocked daily with water and soft drinks, and above the fridge a range of small, exquisitely hand-carved cupboards.

In one of the cupboards was a comprehensive first aid kit and Leandro deposited her gently on a sofa in the sitting area, with orders to stay seated, while he fetched it. He also got a bowl of water from the kitchen and a face towel from the bathroom. En route, he noticed the bed—the indentation of her head on the pillow, the shoes casually kicked off and lying on the ground, the clothes over the back of the chair. She might give the impression of being Miss Prim and Proper, but the air of charming disorder in the room told a different story. He spotted, in passing, a bra hooked over the cupboard handle and half smiled—because that, if anything, was the sort of undergarment he associated with her. Plain, white, simple...

'Okay...'

'Honestly, Leandro, this is totally unnecessary. I can handle a little cut.'

'You're lucky you didn't twist your ankle. I'll have to make sure that the routes back to the cabanas are more adequately lit.'

'You mean for those foolhardy guests who have too much to drink?'

Her voice sounded unnaturally high, but then how could it not when he was kneeling like a supplicant at her feet, gently removing her sandal so that he could soak her injured foot in the warm water in the small basin he had managed to find in the kitchen? The feel of his hands on her skin made her tremble. Who would have imagined that such big hands could be so soft and caressing? What would it be like to have them caress her everywhere? To have them trace the contours of her naked body…every indentation?

She had to suppress a shameless urge to groan aloud just at the thought of it.

How had she ended up in this place? Engaged to a man for reasons no one should be, and stupidly drawn to another when she knew the attraction was not only futile but also sliced through every notion she had ever had about men who played around? Men who didn't know the meaning of the word commitment? Men who ruined other people's lives…?

But he never led them on…he never made promises he couldn't deliver…

His words came back to her in a contradictory rush and she blocked her mind off to them.

'Haven't you ever been…foolhardy?' he asked softly. 'Had a little too much to drink? Said a few things…done a few things…that you semi-regretted in the morning?'

He looked straight at her before she had time to avert her eyes and she reddened.

'Not that I can recall,' she muttered uncomfortably.

Leandro sat back on his haunches with her foot still in his hand. 'Really?'

Emily tugged her leg and he returned his attention to sorting out the cut on her foot. It was a simple matter of cleaning the wound and applying a bandage. In fact, it barely needed a bandage at all, but he was taking his time. She had, he noticed, remarkably slim ankles and beautifully shaped feet, her toenails neat and short.

'I've always been a very careful person. I'm not sure I'll be able to go on a sightseeing tour with you tomorrow, Leandro. Not with my…damaged foot… Walking will probably be difficult…'

'Always?'

'Sorry?' Emily was temporarily confused.

'You said that you've *always* been a careful person...'

He sat back and inspected his handiwork with a critically appreciative eye. Neatly bandaged, neatly cleaned.

He levered himself up and before she could protest he was sitting on the sofa next to her, depressing it with his weight, far too close to her for his liking.

'Aren't you a bit too young to be careful *all the time*?'

'I'm just not inclined to take risks,' Emily returned defensively.

And was her engagement part of that pattern of not taking risks? Leandro wondered. Had she decided on a safe bet? Someone who didn't set her world alight because having her world set alight would be taking a risk, and she didn't do risk-taking? Was that why she was so tight-lipped when it came to discussing the one thing in her life that she should have been shouting from the rooftops?

He remembered that feeling he had had—that feeling that she was *aware* of him, aware of him as a man...

In his head, strands of information were rearranging themselves, reconfiguring into bite-sized pieces he could deal with,—bite-sized pieces that made perfect sense as soon as he began thinking laterally, as he was now doing.

She didn't love the guy she was engaged to. When she spoke about him it was with reticence and a certain amount of caution. Maybe she liked the man, but more likely she simply saw him as a rescue package because she feared entering her thirties without a partner and he was a safe bet—someone from her childhood who had resurfaced. He didn't challenge her, but neither did he repel her. The poor guy was probably besotted with her. She had cool, eye-catching killer looks. Doubtless he fancied himself in love and she was going along for the ride because something was better than nothing.

The thought that she might be attracted to *him* appealed to a part of Leandro that was instinctive and primal and intensely satisfying.

'I don't think your foot should come between you and a relaxing day exploring the island,' he murmured, with a slow, lazy smile that she found vaguely disconcerting. 'I've cleaned all the blood, and I'm pleased to tell you that it's a surface cut only. In fact barely in need of a bandage. But, as a careful person, you'll appreciate that it's better to be safe than sorry…'

'There's nothing wrong with being careful.' Emily felt drawn to justify herself. 'You apply that to all your work dealings…'

'Ah, but that's where it ends.'

'Is it? I thought you were very careful not to get too involved in your personal relationships,' she answered with asperity, and then flushed—because what was the point in trying to resurrect barriers only to trample them underfoot the second she was drawn into a non-work-related conversation with him?

'*Touché*—although I'm not sure your comparison is valid.'

'What time do you anticipate we will be leaving in the morning for this sightseeing tour?' Emily couldn't meet his eyes. She could still feel the sensation of his hands on her foot and her body was still tingling from thoughts that had no place in her head. 'If I'm up to it.'

'You'll be up to it.' Leandro stood up, returned the basin to the small kitchen and then strolled to the window to gaze briefly out into the darkness before turning to face her. 'I'll get Antoine to prepare a picnic for us…'

'Is that really necessary? We could always return here to the hotel…'

'We'll be out for the day, Emily,' Leandro said gently.

'Back late afternoon. It may be a small island, but there's no rush, is there? And…' He paused and allowed his eyes a leisurely roam. 'Avoid the starchy clothing. Swimsuit, towel, sunblock…you won't need any more than that…'

CHAPTER FIVE

EMILY COULDN'T REMEMBER the last time she had been on holiday. Any holiday of any kind, barring the good old and bitterly remembered days when she had still been caught up in the illusion of happy family life. When her parents had taken her abroad on expensive holidays to expensive destinations. Those didn't count. And for the better part of her adult life...well, there had been no opportunity, no money, no time...and hardly any inclination when she thought about it.

Now, as she stood in front of the mirror and contemplated the girl staring back at her, she was disturbed to find that she felt in a holiday mood. The warmth, the salty smell of the sea, the uninterrupted sound of waves lapping against a shoreline, the lack of crowds which imposed an atmosphere of serenity and intimacy...

Sometimes it was hard to drag herself back to the reality of the situation. That she was here because of work—because she had handed in her notice—because he didn't trust her not to fly to his competitors and divulge state secrets. Or maybe simply because it was within his power to make her stay and complete her full notice, so he would.

And as soon as she began thinking that she likewise remembered *why* she had handed in her notice. Because her life was about to change. Because she was going to get married. To Oliver. For reasons which were complex and cynical and somehow made her feel immeasurably sad. But when she felt herself spiralling down that road she always managed to yank herself away from the brink.

Except now—right now, right here—with the windows to the cabana flung open on a view of lush, breathtaking, Technicolor beauty, she could feel dissatisfaction creep up on her. Dissatisfaction and melancholy at where her life was going. She would never experience this again—this feeling of simmering excitement because she was looking forward to a day out. With a guy who...

She turned away abruptly from the full-length mirror and flung her towel, her sunblock, a tee shirt and a pair of shorts, her book and her hat into the colourful canvas beach bag she had been tempted into buying from the hotel shop.

Her foot was completely fine and she had removed the bandage and replaced it with a strip of plaster. It felt odd to leave her laptop behind, charging on the desk in the little sitting room. She had so far managed to tote it along everywhere with her, like a solid, tangible shield against personal contact with Leandro. Fat lot of good it had done her.

Here she was with her hair swinging down her back in a plait, dressed in shorts and a tee shirt like a teenager, with her sensible swimsuit underneath and a simmering sense of excitement when she should have been feeling apprehensive and resentful at spending the day in his company.

She had eaten breakfast in her bedroom and spotted Leandro as soon as she entered the reception area of the hotel. Everyone was gearing up for the big photo shoot. There was a general air of excitement. The casual clothing of the staff which had been in evidence previously had been jettisoned in favour of uniforms: crisp white and mint-green. Amidst all this Leandro cut a commanding figure, surrounded by some of his employees who were hanging onto his every word.

Her heart skipped a beat as she stood at the side and looked at him. After all this time working for him, spending hours upon hours in his company, she marvelled that she could have kidded herself into believing that he had absolutely no effect on her—that she was immune to his looks. It would seem not. Images of him had obviously been stored in her memory bank, and now there was no need to be near him to know the way his eyes crinkled when he smiled, the curve of his sexy mouth, the imperious set of his features.

She took a deep breath and walked confidently towards him as the little cluster of dark-skinned, smiling people greeted her and broke away, scurrying off in different directions.

'They're thrilled with all of this, aren't they?' Emily asked politely.

She had to stop herself from staring at him. He was wearing a pale blue polo shirt and khaki shorts that showed off the length and strength of his muscular legs, liberally sprinkled with dark hair.

'Wouldn't you be?' Leandro looked down at her—at the impossibly fair hair, the long, slender legs, the sexy, boyish physique. She looked incredibly young without the suit, without make-up, without the severe hairstyle.

'I guess so.' Emily laughed, eyes carefully averted, shielded with one hand against the blinding glare of the camera flashes. 'How long will they be here?'

'Wrapped up in a day. We should miss the thick of it. Unless, of course, you'd like to be photographed for the spread?'

'Absolutely not!'

'Why not?' Leandro drawled. 'Are you camera-shy? No need, you know. I imagine you're incredibly photogenic...'

Emily reddened and wondered whether this was a flirtatious remark—then immediately chided herself for being over-imaginative. This was just how he was. Innately charming. It was why women found him so irresistible. It was why...

The natural conclusion of this train of thinking should have been her being led down a well-trodden and familiar path. Innately charming, irresistible—hence womaniser and general player whose modus operandi involved breaking hearts.

However, she lost the thought before she could follow it through. She was too busy playing with the idea that he found her photogenic.

She tripped along behind him towards a buggy which was only slightly bigger than a motorised golf cart and handed him her bag, which he tossed into the back seat, where it joined a massive picnic basket and a cooler containing, she assumed, an assortment of cold drinks.

'Do you know how to drive this thing?' She hesitated as he held the door open for her.

'If I can fly a plane then I can certainly drive this little motorised tin can. Besides, there's no traffic to speak of around here, and you have my word that I will protect you as though my life depended on it.'

Emily felt another quiver of *something*—something that made her feel hot and flustered and a little bit scared.

'I hope you've brought your sunblock?' He glanced across at her as he swung himself into the driver's seat and reversed the buggy at alarming speed, sending up a little flurry of gravel. 'You look like you burn easily.'

'I'll be fine, thank you.'

'You're already a little sunburned on the bridge of your nose.'

Emily automatically rubbed her finger along her nose and kept her eyes firmly fixed ahead of her.

'So, tell me what you think of the hotel—how you're enjoying your stay here…'

Having tuned in to those barely visible reactions she had whenever she was in his presence—reactions which he now concluded had always been there, cleverly hidden underneath a polished professional exterior, Leandro now found that they were all he could notice. The way she blushed whenever he surprised her with a remark that was non-work-related, even the most innocuous. The way she looked away, nostrils slightly flared, at the faintest whiff of a *double entendre*.

She fancied him—and where did that leave her so-called fiancé? His curiosity had been aroused and, like an itch, he was determined to scratch it, determined to get to the bottom of the enigma. And playing at the back of his mind was the tantalising notion that if she fancied him—and he was certainly having trouble stamping down his suddenly hectic libido—then where might that lead?

If she figured she was in love with this guy she had jacked her job in for, then wouldn't he be doing her a favour in showing her that that was certainly not the case? Wouldn't he be sparing her a lifetime of unhappiness and regret by demonstrating the unavoidable truth that if she was attracted to other men, specifically *him,* then hitching her wagon to some guy out of desperation was not a solution?

'It's the most beautiful place I've ever been to in my entire life,' Emily answered truthfully. 'The scenery is amazing. So unspoiled. I wonder if the island will remain that way once it's discovered.'

'The minister for tourism here—or for such tourism as exists at the moment—seems to be a very discerning guy.'

Leandro was still caught up in his thoughts, still acutely aware of her sitting so close to him that the smallest shift in his body weight would bring their thighs together.

'He appreciates how important it is to keep the flavour of this island. It's a fine line. Over-development would kill the tourist industry faster than civil war, and he gets that.'

'You're very lucky that you were the first to stamp your mark here…'

'I prefer to think of it as being astute rather than lucky.'

He slid his eyes along to her and inhaled sharply. She was trying and failing in an attempt to keep her hair from flying all over the place as they sped along the small empty road parallel to the sandy strip of coastline. On one side acres of coconut trees meandered towards the town and the outlying suburban areas. On the other more coconut trees separated the road from the beach, and the striking blue of the water could be glimpsed through their slender spiralling trunks. The sky was a perfectly cloudless milky blue. Sea breezes kept the temperature just right, preventing the tropical heat from becoming unbearable. He had chosen the spot for this hotel very carefully.

'Were you always like this?'

'Like what?' Leandro asked, raising his eyebrows in a question.

'Astute when it comes to business?'

'You mean was I doing deals at the age of ten? No. But I inherited the hard-working gene from my father and grew up with the belief that an expensive education was not a right but a privilege—one to be appreciated and used well. And what about you, Emily? Was it always your ambition to be a personal assistant?'

'You say that as though it's something to be…ashamed of.' She turned to him and glared.

'Far from it. Behind every successful businessman

there's always a personal assistant, making sure that all the nuts and bolts are taken care of.'

'I wanted to be a vet,' Emily admitted, because somehow, despite his qualification, he had still managed to make her job sound *pedestrian*. And there was a part of her that wanted him to know that she had once fancied herself as destined for all sorts of things—grand things.

'A vet...' Leandro murmured, and saw her give a curt nod from the corner of his eye. 'That's a far cry from being someone's personal assistant...'

'Yes, it is.'

'Demands high grades...'

'Do you think I wasn't clever enough to get them?'

'Far be it from me to think any such thing. You forget— I've worked with you for nearly two years. I know how clever you are.'

'Now, why does that sound so patronising?' But she laughed and gave up the unequal fight between the wind and her hair. 'I can smell the sea. It's amazing.'

'Look through there—through that clump of trees. Do you see a path? Well, that's where we're going.'

'How on earth do you know about this place?'

'The hotel manager is a fount of information and was only too happy to steer us in the direction of the best beaches.'

He swerved off the road and brought the buggy to a bumpy stop just where the Tarmac gave way to rich soil and the dense, lush foliage that was so much a feature of the tiny island. With the engine killed, the sound of the sea reached her, and she held her face upturned to the sun, enjoying the bliss of the warmth on her skin.

Okay, so it might not be a holiday, but for the first time in as long as she could remember she felt removed from the low-level stress that accompanied her everywhere.

They walked through the roughly hewn path, down a gentle incline and through a bank of coconut trees, emerging onto a strip of sand that was fine, white and powdery. The beach stretched in a half-moon crescent and the sea was as calm as a lake and a piercing turquoise.

Emily stared out, squinting against the sun. She felt free—free from all concerns and worries. She felt like a young woman without a care in the world, and she marvelled that she could have forgotten what that felt like. This was a taste of normality and she savoured it, knowing that its visit would be fleeting.

When she turned around it was to find that Leandro had flung a massive beach rug on the sand and had stripped off to his swimming trunks. The sight of him, bare-chested, was even more breathtaking than the scenery she had been gaping at moments before.

Goodness, had she been fantasising about this all the time she had been working for him? Underneath the blistering scorn and her composed demeanour, had she fooled herself into imagining a detachment that had never been there?

He certainly lived up to any fantasy a girl could have. His shoulders were broad and muscled, his stomach washboard-flat, and the sprinkling of dark hair on his chest was aggressively, challengingly masculine.

She found that she was having trouble breathing, and in a desperate attempt to conceal her shameful reaction reached into the bag over her shoulder and whipped out her sunglasses, which she stuck firmly on the bridge of her nose.

'I take it you're not going to spend the day in shorts and a tee shirt?'

His own clothes had been dumped on the rug, along with the shoes which he had kicked off. Even his feet, she noted distractedly, were unfairly sexy. How was that even possible?

'I'm not a strong swimmer.'

'Don't worry. I'm here. I won't let you be swept away by any treacherous undertows...'

'You're certainly a man of many talents,' Emily bantered uneasily. 'You can fly planes, drive off-road cars and now cross-channel swimming...'

'The cross-channel bit might be taking the talented streak a little far...'

Alert now to her body language, Leandro was feeling the pull of attraction tucked away behind her nervous laughter and light-hearted remarks—and, hell, it had him firing on all cylinders. He folded his arms and tilted his head to one side, his body language redolent of a man waiting. Waiting for her to strip off...

No big deal. Her swimsuit was as daring as a nun's habit. A black one-piece. Yet she was still burning with self-consciousness as she pulled the tee shirt over her head and eased her shorts off, folding both neatly and depositing them on the rug without once glancing in his direction.

'I didn't realise we would be staying in one spot,' she muttered. 'I thought you mentioned exploring the island.'

'And we'll be doing just that.' Leandro began walking towards the water. 'But the drive was just so hot that I thought we could kick off the day with a little swim to cool down. Coming?' He threw the word over his shoulder.

She watched, hesitating, as he waded into the sea and then, when he was quite a long way out, pushed off and began to swim vigorously, until he was just a small speck on the horizon.

Safely far away.

Only then did she venture in. A quick, harmless paddle...

But the water was shallow, and very clear, and amazingly warm. Unable to resist the temptation of actually doing a little proper swimming, she eventually took the plunge. She hadn't been in a public swimming pool, let alone the sea, for as long as she could remember, and although she was an okay swimmer, it was comfortingly reassuring being able to feel the sand under her feet. She flipped over, ducked under the surface, emerged and lay on her back, eyes closed against the glare, arms outstretched as the water lapped around her still body.

She wasn't aware of Leandro slicing through the water towards her until she felt his arms, his body, and in a state of surprised panic she spluttered back to reality, half ducking under before breaking the surface, arms flailing, because the comforting bank of sand was no longer within reaching distance of her toes. And the more she flailed—partly out of surprise at discovering that she had drifted away from the shore, and partly because Leandro's wet proximity was throwing her into a state of mental chaos—the tighter he circled his arms around her.

'Hey! I've got you!'

'And you can let me go! Right now!' She tried to pummel his chest, but that was near impossible given the situation.

'Clasp your arms around my neck, Emily, and we can swim back to shore. You drifted.'

'I'm perfectly…capable…of swimming back unaided!'

She gave one final liberating push and began striking back towards the beach, her swimming jerky and frantic.

She waded out angrily. He was right behind her. There was no need for her to turn around to ascertain that fact. What the heck did he think he was playing at?

'I don't appreciate being…being…' When she finally spun round she was safely wrapped up in her towel and breathing so fast that she felt on the verge of hyperventilation.

'Being…?' Leandro drawled silkily.

He took his time sitting down, reaching for his shades,

then stretching himself out on the rug with his legs lightly crossed—the very picture of a man utterly at ease, oblivious to her spluttering anger.

Emily looked at him. She was overreacting. She knew it. She had told him that she wasn't a strong swimmer and she had managed to float her way out of her depth… He had probably fancied himself as lifeguard, saving a damsel about to find herself in distress.

'I'm sorry if you thought I was…in trouble,' she said ungraciously, before quickly remembering that she was still his employee, he was still her boss—even if it didn't feel like that out here, far removed from their daily routine. 'And I appreciate that you thought you needed to save me. I *can* actually swim, Leandro. I just can't enter competitions.'

She wished she could see his eyes, get a handle on how he was reacting, but his dark sunglasses hid everything.

'Why don't you lie down and recover?'

He patted the space next to him without glancing in her direction and Emily looked at his hand with the suspicion of someone eyeing up a deadly snake.

'But don't forget to apply sunblock. I can do without it because I'm dark, but…'

'You don't want the liability of a secretary who can't perform her duties because she has to take to her bed with sunburn?'

Leandro lifted his shades and looked at her evenly. 'For the past year and a half I've wondered what was going through your head. I now realise that you were wrapped up imagining the very worst about me. If you don't want to protect yourself from the sun, then by all means don't.' He replaced his sunglasses and folded his arms on his chest.

She had been dismissed. Along with her churlishness, her childishness, her petty heated responses.

'Have you been to *all* of the beaches on the island?'

She lay down and resumed their conversation in a placatory voice.

Without having to look at him, with only the sky above her to witness her nervous jumpiness, Emily felt a little more at ease.

'I…I suppose you must have had to do a great deal of background checks before you decided to invest your money in this venture…'

'Why did you decide to choose secretarial work over becoming a vet if your grades were good…?'

'I beg your pardon?'

'I visited the island once, shortly before you joined me. I made sure everything and everyone was in place and then I delegated—so, no, I *don't* know every beach on the island. That's your question answered. Now answer mine. Why sit in front of a computer when you could be in the great outdoors, tending to sick animals?'

Leandro didn't need to look at her. He could *sense* her confusion, her unwillingness to run with this conversation. Behind the dark shades his eyes were closed as he allowed the silence to develop between them.

'And don't…' he rolled onto his side and propped himself up on one elbow so that he was now looking at her profile, taking in the way her nostril quivered and her tongue slipped out to moisten her lips '…even *think* of changing the subject…'

Emily kept perfectly still but she could feel his eyes on her. He wasn't going to give up. Perhaps he was bored—perhaps that was what lay behind this curiosity which had never been in evidence before.

His normal weekend in London would have been packed with fun and probably spent in the company of his latest woman. Maybe trawling through overpriced jewellers so that he could let the lucky lady choose something involving diamonds followed by lunch somewhere cool and hip, an afternoon romping in the sack and then something cultured…a night at the opera. The lucky lady might not get to grips with it, but she would certainly appreciate the glamour of the event…

Instead here he was, stuck in Paradise with *her*. His curiosity had been piqued by her resignation, by her tight-lipped responses when questioned, and with nothing better to do on a Saturday, with the sun beating down and none of the usual distractions, the devil was beginning to work on idle hands.

Those semi-flirtatious remarks…the lazy drift of his eyes towards her…standing there the way he had so that he could watch her peel her tee shirt off and strip down to her swimsuit…the relentless way he insisted on dragging their conversation away from the polite and into the murky waters of the personal…

She was leaving his employ. There was no longer any particular need to cultivate distance between them. That worked both ways. Maybe, in the absence of anything better to do, he wanted to have some fun with her.

'I have no idea why you would be interested in my…my past life choices, Leandro!' Emily laughed lightly.

'Call me crazy, but some of us are like that. Interested in other peoples' past life choices…' Not strictly true, of course. He had never been over-curious about any of his girlfriends' past life choices. Perhaps that was because they had always insisted on telling him all about them…

'It was too expensive,' Emily said bluntly.

'Too *expensive*?'

'That's right.' Suddenly restless, she sat up and wrapped her arms around her legs.

Leandro sat up as well, so that they were both now staring out at the glittering sea.

'You probably don't know what it feels like to have to reconsider your options because there's just not enough money in the bank. But some of us do.' And yet, she thought bitterly, it need not have been that way. She should have been able to fulfil her dreams. But instead she had had to resort to a Plan B she had never considered while growing up.

'Your family could not have helped you realise your ambitions…?'

'I will not discuss my family.' She glanced across to him with a cool, unreadable expression.

He was locked out. It was as if the shutters had dropped, sealing off all points of entry. Why wouldn't she discuss her family? What was so taboo about that? But then, what was so taboo about discussing her engagement? Clearly quite a lot.

'Well, then,' he drawled with lazy insistence, 'why don't we discuss your boyfriend?'

He turned to face her and removed his shades. Then he reached forward and removed hers. Just like that. Before she had time to take preventative measures. Before she could pull back from feeling the touch of his fingers on her face.

'I thought we'd covered that topic already.' She began raising her hand to her face, to brush away the feel of his fingers, then thought better of it and lowered it to her side. Instead she stood up and put on her tee shirt before strolling down to the shoreline, just far enough for the warm water to lap over her feet before ebbing away.

Everything about this situation screamed danger, and yet she felt so…so *alive*.

Antennae she hadn't even known she possessed warned her that he was behind her without her having to turn around.

'Have we?' Leandro murmured.

He was standing slightly behind her, the warm breeze whipping her hair against him, and his fingers itched to reach out and yank that little blue elastic band out of her hair so that he could appreciate it loose and unencumbered.

'Spoken much to him since we've been here?'

'I don't think that's any of your business,' Emily blustered.

'Missed him much?'

'How dare you ask questions like that?' She spun round to look at him and immediately regretted it because she was now only inches away from him. The broad, naked width of his powerful chest confronted her like an implacable wall. 'And…and…*can't you put on a tee shirt?*'

'Why? Does it bother you seeing me like this?'

'Of course it doesn't!'

'So why would I want to put anything on? It's hot.'

'We should be thinking of carrying on with this tour,' Emily said agitatedly. 'We'll never cover the island at this rate.'

'The island is the size of a postage stamp. Trust me. We can stay here for another hour and still cover it twice over before dark. The reason I ask whether you're pining for your one true love is because I don't think you are.'

'I beg your pardon?'

'You heard me, Emily. You haven't mentioned the man once since we've been here.'

'I'm an extremely private person. You know that.'

'So private that when Nigel Sabga, the hotel manager, asked you whether you were married you told him that you didn't believe in marriage?'

'You were *eavesdropping* on our conversation?' It had been a question asked in passing and answered truthfully and without thought. But then, she hadn't realised that Leandro had been lurking behind a wall somewhere, ear-wigging.

'You probably didn't see me. I was sampling some of the wines behind a screen in the dining area.'

He stared at her until she felt hot colour crawl into her cheeks.

'So… Peculiar remark, wouldn't you say? For someone about to tie the knot with the love of their life? But then, I don't imagine he *is* the love of your life.'

'You don't know what you're talking about, and you have no right to…to…'

'Of course I have no right!' Leandro shrugged his shoulders with eloquent nonchalance. 'But you're soon to be my ex-employee. All bets are off when it comes to walking carefully round one another. Why are you marrying the guy if you don't believe in marriage? Are you scared of ending up on your own? You shouldn't be. You're not old enough to have such fears…'

'Of course I'm not scared of ending up on my own,' Emily retorted scornfully. 'Why should I be?'

'Who knows how you feel on the subject?' He paused, dark eyes still fixed on her flushed face. 'After all, you're marrying a guy you clearly don't love, for reasons best known to you, and from what I can see it's not a marriage driven by that other all-important criteria either…'

'I have no idea what you're talking about, Leandro.' Caution and common sense told her to do something—anything rather than stay where she was, like a fly trapped in a spider's web—but her head was refusing to take orders. 'What *"all-important criteria"* are you talking about?'

For a few seconds she really was puzzled, but realisation dripped in and she went bright red. Sex. That was what he had been talking about. What else?

She tried to activate the appropriate response of disgust

at a man whose mind could only travel down one track, but it seemed that in the space of only a few days he was no longer the one-dimensional figure she had pegged him to be.

She jumped to her feet and began walking restlessly towards the sea, before branching off to explore the rest of the beach and give herself time to harness her chaotic thoughts.

When she sneaked a look over her shoulder it was to find that Leandro had lain back down on the beach rug, hands folded behind his head, sunglasses firmly back in place. The very picture of relaxation.

Emily tightened her lips and continued to walk away from him. If the beach had been longer she would have disappeared and left him to his own devices for as long as she possibly could, but after ten minutes she was forced to stroll back towards him. He had not moved a muscle. Had he even noticed that she had walked away?

'What are you trying to say?' She addressed his prone figure and he lifted his sunglasses to squint up at her.

'Come again?'

Gone was the cool, controlled woman who had performed her duties without once revealing the slightest hint of what went on behind the polite facade. Bit by bit he had witnessed that façade being eroded at the edges, turning her from a statue into a living, breathing woman—a woman with depth and passion and the sort of complexities that could keep a man riveted for a lifetime.

'That remark you made… You know nothing of my relationship with Oliver!'

'I don't have to,' Leandro responded wryly.

He replaced his shades, concealing his eyes, and infuriatingly looked as though he might be on the point of nodding off to sleep in the tropical sun.

'And what does *that* mean?' Irritated, she poked him in his side with her toe.

He caught her foot before she could pull it away.

'I really would avoid doing that,' he drawled, removing the sunglasses to lodge them on the top of his head.

'Or else what?'

Leandro dealt her a slashing smile and kept hold of her foot. 'If you start touching me you might find that I start touching you back…'

Emily's heart slowed and heat suffused her face. She had never been so conscious of her body before—even though he wasn't looking at it, even though his eyes were firmly fixed on her face, even though his expression, despite the innuendo behind his words, was deceptively amused.

'And that's what I'm talking about…' he continued, with silky-smooth intent.

Emily stared at him in silence. She didn't want him to carry on. She really didn't want to hear what he had to say on a subject she had no desire to talk about. But she felt like a rabbit, frozen in the headlights while a car moved inexorably at full speed towards it.

'Ah, I see you get where I'm coming from…'

He sat up and his hand snaked to her wrist, tugging her down beside him so that she half fell onto the rug before shuffling into a sitting position whilst glaring impotently at him.

'The cat is out of the bag, Emily. You're no longer the personal assistant hiding behind a bland exterior with a non-existent private life.'

She was so close to him that he could see the flicker in her eyes…could almost *smell* the scent of an awareness she was desperate to conceal.

'You're engaged to be married to a man for whom you have feelings of…what? Exactly? Certainly not love and—let's be honest, here—definitely not physical attraction. And do you know how I've come to that conclusion?'

He ran his thumb along the side of her cheek in a gesture that was shockingly intimate and she pulled away sharply.

'Point proved. I've come to that conclusion, my dear personal assistant, because you're attracted to *me*...'

CHAPTER SIX

EMILY WAS NOT looking forward to the evening that lay ahead of her, terrifying in its uncertainty, filled with the dreadful potential to do damage in places she least wanted.

'Because...my dear personal assistant...you're attracted to me...'

She recalled Leandro's absolute amused certainty as he had spoken those words, the way his dark eyes had held hers for just a second before roving indolently over her, touching every part of her body until she felt as though she was going to go up in flames.

Of course she had denied any such thing vigorously. She had schooled her features into a mask of disdain. She had reminded him that she had been his secretary for nearly two years, so how, she had asked pointedly, had he only now reached such a ridiculous conclusion? She had informed him coolly that the hot weather must have gone to his head.

Then she had taken refuge in the sea, putting her limited swimming skills to the test and striking out until she'd realised that if she didn't swim back to shore he would probably do something insane, like try and rescue her yet again.

The thought of those strong arms around her had almost made her lose her stride.

He had pulled back the curtain and revealed the monster. The sexual attraction she had been feeling—the one she had tried desperately to conceal—had been exposed and held up for inspection, and even though he had politely allowed the matter to drop she knew that his conclusions had not changed.

They might just as well not have bothered with the trip round the island. She had barely been able to notice a thing. The delicious lunch, eaten in the charming miniature botanical gardens, surrounded by wildly colourful flowers and the sound of birds and insects, had been wasted on her. She had brought her phone with her, thinking that she would capture some of the sights, but in fact she hadn't taken a single picture.

She had been too busy thinking about what he had said and feverishly agonising about the myriad ways he could make the rest of her stay uncomfortable.

She now longed for the safety of those London office walls. She wished that she had avoided this wretched overseas situation by fabricating some kind of clever excuse.

Failing that…

She looked at her reflection and saw, despite the tumultuous churning in her head, the image of a relaxed young woman nothing at all like the expressionless personal assistant who had made a virtue out of being impassive, remote and professional.

She had caught the sun. Despite frequent applications of sunblock her skin was lightly tanned and satin-smooth. Her already fair hair was dazzlingly blonde, lightened by the sun. Forced into summer clothes, her body seemed more exposed than she could ever remember noticing.

She should have been getting a tan for the guy waiting for her back home, but instead she was caught up fighting emotions that had no place in her life, and being apprehensive that somehow those emotions, which she could barely quantify, would take on a life of their own and start demanding attention she couldn't afford to give them.

She would have to return to the topic, like it or not, and dispatch it with a version of the truth—just enough to ensure that things returned to normal. Or as normal as was possible while they were trapped here on Paradise.

She left it as late as possible to join Leandro for dinner. The photo shoot had taken place and she knew that he had been booked for a personal interview and a series of pictures to accompany the article. The last thing she wanted was to be involved and have her picture taken. The entire crew would be staying the night on the hotel compound, sampling the rooms, but an offshore boat had been laid on for them so that they could enjoy dinner out at sea.

Emily thought that they must have fought to get the dream job of a lifetime on this photography stint.

Running nearly an hour late, she found him nursing a drink at the bar, and she faltered before taking a deep breath and walking confidently towards him.

'Am I supposed to consider this fashionably late?' Leandro enquired when she was standing next to him.

She still couldn't quite get used to not seeing him in a suit. Every time she laid eyes on his bare brown arms, his muscular legs, that glimpse of chest visible behind the casual shirt with the top buttons undone, she felt the force of impact anew.

No different now. He was, thankfully, in a pair of long, cool khaki trousers and a dull blue polo shirt, loafers without socks.

'I fell asleep and didn't wake up in time,' Emily lied.

'You've caught the sun.' He beckoned across a waiter and ordered a bottle of wine. 'I thought we could try somewhere different tonight. One of the restaurants in the town.'

'I'd rather stay here,' Emily interjected quickly, because the thought of yet more unchaperoned time with him was the last thing she wanted. 'I'm feeling a little too tired for going out again…'

'Despite the long sleep?'

He marvelled that away from the grey London skies and the impersonal office setting she could have undergone such a dramatic change. The severe hairstyles had all but been abandoned. Instead of her habitual bun she had braided her long vanilla-blonde hair into a loose plait which was draped over one shoulder and tied at the end with a scruffy red elastic band. Devoid of all but the most basic make-up, and wearing no jewellery whatsoever, she still managed to look classier and more tempting than any of the heavily adorned women he was accustomed to dating.

Her dress was a silky flowered shift which exposed as little as possible and yet still managed to get his imagination going.

And that was without thinking back to how she had looked in that unadventurous swimsuit! All long limbs and ballet dancer grace…

He felt the push of an erection and forced it away with difficulty.

'The sun tires me out,' Emily told him vaguely. 'I think I'd spend half my time in bed if I lived over here.'

'Interesting thought.'

Their eyes tangled briefly and she looked away, flushing. There she went again, she thought with annoyance, rising to a bait she wasn't even sure he had consciously planted. Proving to him that what he had said about the whole *attraction thing* was true. An indifferent woman didn't blush whenever there was the slightest bit of innuendo behind a remark!

If she had been with her previous boss, a fatherly type in

his sixties, she would not be trying to fight down the colour invading her cheeks and staring at the bartender with the desperation of a drowning swimmer searching for a life belt in open water.

'How did the photo shoot go?'

'You missed the post-shoot excitement,' Leandro said drily. 'Drinks on the house nearly put paid to their boat trip out to sea. I asked the skipper to make sure the crew kept an eagle eye on the lot of them. *Man overboard!* is not what I want to hear drifting across the water while we're in the middle of our meal.'

Emily smiled reluctantly and cradled the wine in her hand. She allowed herself to be amused by his rendition of the photographer who had tried to get him into various artificial poses, and the journalist covering the feature, who had stumbled over her words and asked him the same question several times.

By the time their starters had been brought to them—casual hors d'oeuvres, because neither of them had the appetite for anything more substantial—they had moved on to a more serious conversation about the effect the article would have on business and then to the wider topic of the effects of tourism in small, undiscovered places.

Even talking shop, she was aware of him in ways she had never been before—or had never *thought* she had been before.

Almost without her being aware of it, her eyes took in the smallest changes in his expression, the movement of his hands as he lifted the wineglass to his mouth, the way he had of leaning back in the chair, half smiling, head tilted to one side, listening to her when she said something…

Leandro was beginning to find the work chat tiresome. So many other areas of conversation were up for grabs.

'There's something I feel I ought to tell you,' Emily

began uncomfortably when the wooden board with their starters had been cleared away and there was a lull in the conversation.

'I'm all ears.' Leandro sat forward and looked at her with dark intent. 'Of course if it involves an animated discussion of world events, then I might find my attention drifting…'

'It's always interesting to talk about what's happening in the world,' Emily said. She looked to find, with some surprise, that she had finished her glass of wine and, following the direction of her eyes, Leandro leaned across to pour her a refill.

'I shouldn't,' she murmured, acquiescing.

'Because you might trip again? I might enjoy coming to the rescue… I did last time…'

There was no mistaking the flirtatious innuendo even though his face was perfectly serious, as was his voice.

'I'm not the sort of woman who has time for knights in shining armour,' Emily told him crisply, but she couldn't meet his eyes and instead chose to focus on the attractive displays of hibiscus flowers that dotted the bar counter. 'And *I* happen to find world events fascinating. I guess, from what you're saying, it's not the sort of thing you like talking about with the opposite sex!'

'I can't say I have known many of them who would have had the remotest clue as to what was happening outside their immediate range of vision.' Leandro raised his eyebrows with wry amusement. 'So what you're telling me is that the boyfriend isn't your knight in shining armour?'

'I understand why you're curious about my…my situation…' Emily mumbled. 'I know you think that I should be more…excited…about the whole getting married thing…'

'Ah…' Leandro settled back and waited for her to continue. 'It all seems a bit sudden,' he prompted as the silence lengthened.

Out of the corner of his eye he could see their food being brought over to them with all the smiling enthusiasm he had taken note of over the past few days. It couldn't be happening at a worse time. He didn't want her to retreat behind any more banalities about the state of the world.

Restlessly he waited as platters of food were placed in front of them. Fresh fish, plantain, plates of local sweet potatoes, yam and aubergine.

'You were saying...?' He resumed the conversation when the waiter had faded away. He was keenly aware of her deliberate attempt to avoid catching his eye. Curiosity ripped through him—not a mild stirring of interest, but a sharp, biting feeling that raced through his veins like a shot of pure adrenaline.

'Oliver and I go back a long way...' She cleared her throat, focusing on how she could placate his inquisitiveness with just enough of an explanation. 'I mean, he's been abroad working, but when he returned we picked things up...'

'Picked what up? Hot sex?'

'We don't *all* see sex as an answer to everything.'

'I'm curious as to why you're with the man.'

'It's something of an arrangement,' Emily told him, without inflection in her voice. 'Something that suits us both. We get along fine with one another...'

'You're marrying for convenience because you *"get along"*? There must be more to it than that.'

'I'm not into romance,' she said with a trace of bitterness in her voice. 'I'm into...security...'

'Explain.'

'There *are* no more explanations, Leandro,' she told him pleadingly. 'I'm your secretary. I don't have to answer these questions, but I'm doing it because I know you're curious and I know what you're like. You won't give up and we're stuck here...'

She concentrated on the food on her plate and felt his eyes on her, burning a hole straight to the deepest part of her where her thoughts were hidden.

'So what do we do about this situation?' Leandro drawled, closing his knife and fork on yet another fantastic meal.

'Well, I will, of course, carry on working for you until my notice is up. I'll try and source my replacement before I leave, obviously, but if I can't find anyone you're satisfied with, then I'm going to leave anyway.'

'I wouldn't have it any other way!' He spread wide his arms in a gesture of magnanimous generosity. 'Let's go for a walk on the beach.'

'I beg your pardon?'

'It's an exquisite night. Do you hear the insects just above the sound of the water lapping on the shore?' He allowed her a few seconds to appreciate the imagery. He hadn't been aware that he had such a poetic streak to his personality.

'A—a walk?' Emily stammered.

'Or a dip in the sea. There's something special about swimming at night.'

'I definitely won't be doing *that*!' Emily said, horrified at the idea.

'That's fine. We'll settle for just the walk, in that case...'

She wondered how she had managed to be railroaded into this when, fifteen minutes later, she was standing on the beach with him. There was a slight breeze, but nothing to deflect the warmth of the night. The sky was clear, with the stars out, and the sea was just a silvery body of water.

Leandro had rolled up his trouser legs and kicked off his

shoes, which were lying somewhere by the little outcrop of rocks leading up to the hotel gardens.

'You'll need to take those sandals off,' he suggested, turning around to look at her, a tall, dark, shadowy looming mass of pure muscle and undefined, exciting threat. 'There's nothing worse than sand in your shoes. Very uncomfortable.'

Reluctantly Emily slipped off the sandals and dangled them in one hand. Leandro reached out, removed them from her loose grasp and tossed them in the general direction of where his own shoes were.

'Don't worry, they'll be fine. Enjoy the sensation of sand between your toes.'

The hotel beach was long and unspoiled. As the hotel compound was left behind them the broad strip of sand, banked on one side by the dark water and on the other by an equally dark mass of tightly packed coconut trees, assumed a strangely intimate air.

Jittery, Emily lurched into an awkward, stilted conversation about something trivial she had read about online that was happening back in England. A dreary story concerning two celebrities and an on-screen feud that had ended in fisticuffs. After Leandro's amused remarks about his girlfriends taking no interest in world affairs she had felt suddenly dreary and dull and pedestrian in her interest in what was happening on the big stage, although trying to raise a laugh about a ridiculous piece of showbiz gossip hardly seemed an improvement now.

She petered out into awkward silence and only realised that he had stopped walking when she glanced sideways to find no one next to her.

Bemused, she turned around and looked at him. He was standing perfectly still, arms folded. In the darkness there was no way that she could decipher the expression on his face.

'So…' he drawled.

'So?' She felt a little shiver ripple through her body, and of their own accord her disobedient legs jerked into action and headed slowly in his direction, until she was standing right in front of him, staring up into his dangerously sexy face.

'What are we going to do about our…little situation…?'

'What situation are you talking about?'

'You know exactly what I'm talking about, my dear secretary.' A light gust blew some strands of hair across her face and he brushed them back and then kept his hand where it was, by her ear, which he proceeded to caress idly.

Emily had never experienced anything quite so erotic in her life before.

She had been in two relationships—if they could be called relationships—in all her twenty-seven years.

The first when she was nineteen, with a boy she had convinced herself she fancied because he fancied her, and his enthusiastic pursuit had broken down her natural caution. But the spark had been missing and it had eventually fizzled out into a nondescript friendship which, in turn, had disappeared in the mists of time. She had no idea what had happened to him.

The second, four years later, had been a similar disaster, she knew at least in part driven by her guilty knowledge that she was young and couldn't live the rest of her life in nun-like celibacy. A little tipsy, she had gone back to his place. Yet again there had been no spark, and they had returned to the point from which they had started. Just friends.

And since then…nothing.

Except, she considered with painful awareness, life had

not been quite a desert of cobwebs gathering on her sexuality, had it? Because she had to admit grudgingly that beneath the contempt she had strenuously told herself she felt for her wretched boss there had been something else. Something that had put a spring in her step every morning when she had set off for work—something that had made her never resent it when she had been asked to work ridiculously long hours…when she had been cooped up with him as he nailed down one of his legendary deals…

And now here she was. She could feel herself staring up at him for an inappropriately long time, barely breathing, drawn irresistibly like a moth to a flame.

'Do I?' she croaked, defending herself with what little was left in her armoury. She was so hotly aware of that absent-minded caress on her ear that she felt she might faint.

'Of course you do,' Leandro asserted, in the voice of someone stating the obvious.

He dropped his hand and began walking, so that she fell in step with him. He could feel her presence beside him, nervous, quivering, and yet she was driven to remain even if a part of her might be telling her to flee back to the safety of the hotel.

'You're getting married for reasons that escape me,' Leandro murmured. 'You're not attracted to the man and you don't love him… Okay, security might be an appealing part of the deal, but I honestly can't think that it would constitute reason enough…'

'I never said that I didn't love—'

'Of course you did.'

'Stop pretending that you know what's going on in my head!'

'An *arrangement*. Isn't that what you called it?'

Emily heard the hard edge in his voice and cringed. Put like that, it sounded…sordid. At best. And yet he

didn't know the half of it. But it wasn't his business!
None of it was!

'There's nothing wrong with an arranged marriage,' she
muttered impotently. 'It happens. Some people might say
that the most successful marriages are the ones that are
made for sensible, practical reasons.'

'And you're one of those people...?'

'You're a practical man. You can see where I'm coming
from!' There was a desperate, pleading tone to her voice
that made her cringe inwardly.

How had she got to this point? Girls should have dreams,
shouldn't they? She never had. Not as far as she could remember. Or maybe her dreams were so far in the past that
she could scarcely remember the sensation of having them,
of ever having dreamt of the walk up the aisle, the blushing bride dressed in white, bursting with happiness and
anticipation.

'I'm practical, Emily, but when it comes to the insti-
tution of marriage I still believe in it. I would no sooner
dream of arranging a marriage for myself because it suited
me for practical reasons than I would consider freefalling
off the side of a building without a harness. Of course...'
He thought of his one failed gold-digger mistake. 'I would
be sensible when it came to choosing a woman... I would
pay particular attention to the fact that people from similar
backgrounds tend to forge lasting relationships. But within
those parameters...well...a marriage without love and good
sex as a foundation is a marriage without a point.'

'Well, we can't all be the same, can we?' Emily muttered, breaking their intense eye connection to spin away
and begin walking shakily towards the far end of the beach.

The further they walked away from the hotel, the darker
the beach and their surroundings became. The strip of sand
narrowed towards the end, tailing off into an outcrop of

dramatic rocks of different shapes and sizes—some towering upwards, others flat and squat—and between them the sea surged and fell back in a repeated motion, sending up flicks of spray as it did so.

Emily turned away from the dark mass of menacing rock to find that Leandro was right there, a few paces behind her, just as menacing.

With a sigh of pure frustration she headed towards the trees and sat down on a fallen trunk that lay on the beach like the body of a long, slender, inert snake.

She drew her legs up and folded her arms around them, resting her chin on her knees and staring sightlessly out to the ocean as he sat heavily next to her.

'I believe in marriage because I had the example of my parents,' Leandro said slowly. 'So, whilst I might fool around with women, like I say, they always know the score. And when the time comes for me to marry my head might play a part, but I intend to do it for all the right reasons. So tell me, Emily, how is it that you have no such illusions that it's possible for two people to marry because they actually believe in love…?'

Emily didn't say anything. If anyone had told her two months ago…two *weeks* ago for that matter…that she would be sitting on a beach having a conversation with her boss that defied all rules of propriety, she would have laughed in disbelief.

'It occurs to me that I don't know a damn thing about your background…' Leandro broke his own rule of allowing silence to propel a conversation. He raked his fingers through his hair.

'Why would you?' Emily finally volunteered. 'Updating you on my background was never part of my job description.'

'And you were always so damned efficient when it came

to sticking strictly to the job description and never putting
a foot out of line… So here's what I'm thinking: you don't
believe in marriage and you don't believe in the fairytale
concept of falling in love because of something that happened to you in the past. Either a disastrous relationship
with some guy or else your family background…something
there… Tell me if I'm heading in the right direction with
either of those theories…'

'I don't have to tell you anything,' Emily protested
weakly.

'But there's where you're wrong. Because you've just
been thrown a curve ball in your neatly arranged plans for
your neatly arranged marriage to this mystery guy who
does nothing for you but apparently fits the bill because
he's *convenient*.'

Emily turned to stare at him. His eyes glittered in the
darkness. She could *sense* the dangerous intent inside him
even though his body language was relaxed and casual, his
arms resting loosely on his knees.

'What curve ball?'

'Why, us, of course. You and me and the sizzling flare
of attraction we feel for one another. And don't bother trying to deny it, Emily. Maybe it was there lurking all along
and it took this…'

He looked around him and she knew that he was not only
referring to the lush tropical setting but to the fact that they
were so far removed from the comfort blanket of surroundings with which they had always been familiar and which
had always imposed strict guidelines to their interaction.

He returned his dark gaze to her mesmerised face. '…to
bring it out into the open. But there you go. It's out in the
open. Maybe I would have forced it back into the box if I
had believed for one second that you were truly in love with
your fiancé, but you're not, and that explains why you're

drawn to me just as I'm drawn to you… What you have might be convenient, but it's no protection when it comes to the pull of raw, physical sexual chemistry, is it…?'

Raw…physical…sexual…chemistry… Just those four words, verbalising what had been going on between them underneath the surface, sent a slow, rolling tidal wave of intense excitement coursing through her body. Suddenly breathing was difficult, and she was vibrantly aware of every part of her body, from her tingling nipples to the dampness between her legs, wetting her underwear, making her want to shift and squirm.

'My father…' She rushed desperately into speech, terrified that her body was going to let her down and vaguely aware that she had never felt anything like this for any man in her life before. Although she knew she could never, ever *like* Leandro, despite what he had said about his fair treatment of women, she still didn't want to go there. Or rather she knew, just *knew,* that she shouldn't.

'Your father…?' Leandro was so focused on what his own body was doing and the heat between them that it took him a few seconds to latch on to this surprising turn in the conversation.

'When I was fourteen I found out that he had been unfaithful to my mother…' Her voice hitched. This was a story she had never related to anyone before. She felt as if she was buying time, sharing this confidence, *putting off the inevitable…*

She firmly clamped her brain shut on that alarming thought.

'I'm sorry. That must have been tough on you. Fourteen is an impressionable age.'

'Some of us were flying planes solo and others were… yes…dealing with other things…' She smiled wryly.

His gentle tone of voice had disarmed her, but then

hadn't he been full of surprises since they had got here? Hadn't she reluctantly been forced to see him in a different light? No longer the authoritarian boss but a man who could be thoughtful in his dealings with the locals, shrewd with their concerns, ambitious on their behalf?

The way he had left his guy in charge of the entire photo shoot, allowing the man to take on the responsibility, while he, Leandro, disappeared tactfully for the day… Even though it was, in the end, an important event that could have a significant impact on the hotel either way.

'If it had been a normal case of infidelity things might have been different.' Emily shrugged. She had thought to have boxed the past up and sealed it away, but now it felt as though it had been lying very close to the surface indeed, controlling her behaviour and taking charge of her actions without her even realising.

Leandro listened, his head tilted to one side. He had never encouraged too many confidences in the women he dated. He had always seen that as a step through a door he did not wish to open—a door that would remain firmly shut until the right woman came along—a step towards giving them ideas that weren't justified. But this one woman had hardly been an open book over the past two years, and the fact that she was opening up now did something to him— roused him in a way he couldn't quite put a finger on.

'I mean, loads of kids grow up with warring parents, and so when a divorce happens they're braced for it. My parents never fought. They were a model couple. My father was always attentive, so when it happened it was like a bolt of thunder on a clear summer day. It was just after Christmas—beginning of January. My mother had the crazy idea to do some spring cleaning. Dad was away and she thought she'd have a go at his office.'

She banked down a stupid rush of tears at the memory.

'I remember she was singing along to something on the radio and then there was silence…and silence… When I finally clocked that and popped in she was curled up on the floor, whimpering. There were photos all around her. Photos of a young Thai girl. With Dad and with a toddler. To cut a long story short, it turned out that the perfect husband and the perfect dad had been having an affair with this girl he'd met in a bar in Bangkok. For over five years. While my mum had been keeping the house in order and looking after me, patiently waiting for him to return from his so-called working trips abroad, he had been leading a double life. In an instant everything I'd relied on was blown apart.'

Her lips thinned into a line of bitterness.

'It all came out in the wash, of course. He confessed to everything. Not only had the woman had his child, but at the time all of this was exposed she was seven months pregnant with their second. In a heartbeat my father went from being a man I loved and respected to a stranger who was repellent and disgusting.'

'That's…awful…' Indeed Leandro could barely get his head round the enormity of such betrayal and how it must have affected an impressionable teenager.

Emily looked at him and relaxed, because what she saw on his face was genuine concern and sympathy and it felt as if those were two things she had never had before when it came to her past, because the story had never been told.

'Is she still alive…?'

'Yes.' Emily glanced down, because that was where the story ended as far as Leandro was concerned.

'And along the way you came to the conclusion that relationships with men were not to be relied upon…?'

'We all have learning curves,' she said with a shrug. 'Mine just came a little earlier and a little harder than most.'

'So you're going to settle with a guy who makes you feel

safe because if you don't give anything to him then you can't get hurt.' When she didn't say anything, he continued, changing tactic, 'And can I ask where your father is now?'

'Don't know, don't care.' One hundred per cent true.

'Marry this guy,' Leandro said slowly, 'and you build a prison for yourself.'

'I don't care what you think.'

'You've forgotten what it is to trust because of past experience…and you've got it into your head that I'm just the sort of unreliable player who uses women merely because I have a healthy sex life…'

Emily's eyes dropped to his beautiful mouth and her thoughts became muddled and uncertain. She was only aware of the sexy curve of his lips, the beauty of his face, the leashed masculine power of his body.

'Like I said, I might have fun with women but I don't conform to being the kind of man who could ever do what your father did. The thought of it repulses me on every level. I think you're making a mistake, marrying this guy of yours for the wrong reasons, but in the meantime, before you settle down to a life of predictable mediocrity, why don't you take a little time out to live a little, to let your passion rule your head…?'

Emily was vaguely thinking that he had barely skirted round the real reason she was marrying Oliver. If only he knew the steps she had been prepared to take—because, yes, if you didn't give anything to a man, then how could you end up getting hurt?

'I would never touch another man's woman,' he murmured, reaching to stroke her cheek, 'but then again…'

His mouth met hers and he was temporarily lost, drowning in the most amazing sensation of having his kiss returned, tentatively at first, then with more of that passion he had sensed lurking below the surface.

He broke apart, breathing heavily. 'You're no man's woman, are you...?'

CHAPTER SEVEN

'PLEASE...' EMILY PULLED away but her stubborn feet would not let her flee. She remained where she was, staring up at him, trembling like a leaf in a gale, tightly hugging herself in an attempt to impose some order on her runaway thoughts.

'Please...what...?' Leandro enquired softly. 'Please take me right here...? Right now...?'

'No' She took a couple of steps back, trying hard to free herself from the stranglehold of his presence.

'But you want me to...' He closed the small gap she had created. 'And I understand why. You're marrying someone you shouldn't be marrying for reasons that shouldn't exist... You might think you're choosing the safe option but, like it or not, you're attracted to me and you want to explore that. Don't you?'

'Of course I don't!' She spun away, headed down to the water's edge and felt the sea curl around her feet then ebb away. She could feel him approaching her, darkly and dangerously persistent.

She *could* sleep with him. Oliver wouldn't mind. In fact he would probably applaud it. She could snatch this experience and see what it felt like to have sex with a man she was violently attracted to. It would be a first.

She stiffened when she felt his hands firmly on her shoulders.

Her thoughts were all over the place. Love was an illusion—something she could never believe in and would never fall for—but lust...

She was only finding out now that that was as real as the ocean spreading out in front of her and as full of terrifying unknowns...

The feel of his mouth against her neck sent a violent shudder through her, because she had not been expecting that. With a will of its own her body curved back against his and she heard the sound of her own soft sigh.

'You want this,' Leandro murmured.

He marvelled that he could keep his voice steady, because his libido was running rampant, doing all sorts of crazy things to his breathing.

'And so do I. But I don't want guilty histrionics afterwards... This is just us...you and me...doing what our bodies are telling us to do before you prance up the aisle with Mr Convenient...'

'I know what you must think of me...' Emily muttered as she slowly turned to face him.

There was so little space between their bodies that she could feel the heat emanating from him. She placed the palm of her hand on his chest and stared up at him. Every nerve, muscle, tendon was straining towards him in anticipation.

'It doesn't matter what I think of you...'

'It does to me!'

'Why?' Leandro bent his head and kissed her slowly, tenderly, prising her mouth open with his tongue and then taking his time to taste her. He could *feel* her hesitancy just as he could *feel* her helpless craving for them to take what had flared up between them through to its logical conclusion.

What *did* he think of her? Did it matter? Sure, she had worked for him for nearly two years, and during that time, when he thought about it, they had developed a curiously close bond, but she would be on her way in the blink of an eye and he wouldn't see her again.

All that mattered was the here and now, and satisfying this physical craving that seemed to have the power of a tsunami.

So she had been affected by a dubious past, by the example of a father who had betrayed his family...?

Was it his concern?

'I'm not one of those women who sleep around...'

'And I'm not one of those men who use women, despite what you think. So why don't we just agree to keep our opinions of each other to ourselves and to just...enjoy...?'

He hitched up her thin summery dress in one quick, smooth motion and the feel of his hands on her waist, underneath the shimmery fabric, nearly induced a fainting fit.

'What do you think about taking a dip naked...?'

'Are you mad?' Her heart was beating so fast that she couldn't catch her breath properly.

'I shall have to work on that unadventurous streak in you, my dear secretary...'

'Please don't call me that. It reminds me of how crazy this is...it reminds me that you're my boss and I didn't come here to...to...'

'Have wild, passionate sex with me...?'

'Something like that,' Emily muttered.

The liquid pooling between her legs made her fidget and, as if knowing precisely what was going on with her body, he dipped his hand lower, leaving it poised tantalisingly over her lacy underwear, a delicious promise of what she might expect.

'So you won't be fulfilling my fantasies by dressing in your very best work outfit so that I can rip it all off you...?'

The picture he painted was horribly evocative. She had a vivid mental image of herself back in London, in the office, with the door shut as he tore her clothes off before making love to her sprawled across his big desk.

'Never mind.'

Leandro slipped his finger underneath the top of her underwear and lazily stroked her. He delighted in the feel of the downy hair. In fact it was a massive turn-on—and not just because touching her was beginning to make him think that he had been fantasising about it for longer than he cared to admit to himself.

No, that patch of hair was a sexy reminder that *this* was what a woman should feel like, as opposed to the fashionable baby-smoothness he was accustomed to.

He wanted to burrow and nuzzle against her, breathe in and taste the honeyed wetness between her legs, but instinct told him that he couldn't rush things. He didn't want her running away.

She might be marrying for the wrong reasons, might feel nothing but mild affection for her husband-to-be, but somewhere there must still be a conscience telling her that what she was doing was not exactly morally acceptable.

Fortunately that wasn't his problem. He had given her conscience an out clause but he still didn't want her to suddenly decide to take it...not when he was burning up for her, his body raging with need and desire...

He slipped his fingers underneath the lacy briefs and along her crease, seeking out the slippery nub of her clitoris, wanting to play with it until she was begging him to carry on, until her mind was for him and him alone.

Emily gasped. She arched back and gripped his shoulders. They were still fully clothed and there was something wickedly decadent about that—something that made his finger rubbing against her feel shockingly, *wonderfully* intimate.

Leandro curled his free hand into her hair and titled her head back at just the right angle so that he could kiss her senseless, barely giving her the opportunity to surface for air.

'Enjoying yourself?' His voice was a husky murmur and Emily nodded on a groan. 'Do you,' he grunted, against his better judgement, 'feel unfaithful to the man you're about to engage with in joyous wedlock?'

'Please, Leandro…' she panted as he began to rub his finger against her, bringing her to soaring heights before slowing the pace so that she could catch her breath and try and get her brain working.

'*Do* you?'

'No,' Emily whispered. 'I told you… Our relationship… We… It's not physical…'

Not physical yet…

'Shall we go back to the hotel?' he murmured huskily. 'You don't want a midnight swim in the ocean with me, and my practical streak is telling me that making love on the sand might get a little…uncomfortable. When I enjoy you, I want to enjoy you without the distraction of any discomfort…'

Without warning, he swept her off her feet and began walking back in the direction of the hotel.

Emily squealed.

'People will see us, Leandro!'

'Oh, the joy of owning this place. I don't care. I'm sure tongues are already wagging anyway…'

'You haven't said anything, have you?' she asked,

alarmed, and she heard the wicked grin in his voice when he replied.

'I don't have to. Any idiot would have been able to notice the way I've been looking at you for the past few days.'

'*I* haven't.'

'That's because you've been busy trying to keep your eyes off me.'

'I can't imagine what you must think of me,' she muttered against his chest.

She could well imagine. A woman with no moral scruples. A woman who was happy to sleep with her boss while making wedding plans to marry another man. She might have sketched out some of the truth behind her relationship with Oliver—and who knew? Leandro might well have bought it—but she had to admit to herself that he wasn't quite the cad she had always imagined him to be.

She felt that she had deliberately chosen to see the superficial side to him—to see the man who played the field, picking up women and dumping them without a backward glance.

She had never questioned his ethics. Instead she had chosen to equate them with the ethics of her father. She hadn't stopped to consider that Leandro was simply a single red-blooded male who was free to have affairs and to enjoy the single life—unlike her father, who had been married, with a child, and had chosen to fool around in the most despicable fashion behind his wife's back. Where her father had made a career out of deceit and lies, Leandro had promised nothing to the women he had dated.

At heart, he was far more of a romantic than she was, and while that should have absolved her from feeling any guilt she was still overwhelmed by it as he nudged open the door to his cabana and carried her to his bed.

His room was similar to hers, with variations in the

colour scheme and in the local paintings on the wall over the bed. Flowers in her room…birds in his.

She allowed herself a few seconds of distraction, looking around her curiously, registering the clothes neatly folded on a chair—obviously part of room service and tidied by one of the hotel cleaners. She imagined that he was not a man who spent much time keeping his surroundings pristine.

Inevitably, though, her eyes returned to him, to where he was standing at the foot of the bed with one hand on the button of his trousers.

'You were saying…?' Leandro drawled, not making a move towards her.

'What was I saying?'

'I think your conscience was beginning to act up…'

'I didn't think you'd heard.'

'I heard. You want to succumb to a change of mind, Emily? You're free to go. I've always made it a rule never to get into bed with any woman who didn't want to be there.'

'I bet you haven't had anyone who didn't.'

'Are you about to spoil my record? If you are, tell me and I'll get the cold shower running.'

Automatically her eyes skimmed the bulge in his trousers that was vibrant proof of how aroused he was, and all over again her thoughts went into meltdown.

So who cared what he thought of her? They weren't about to embark on a soul-searching relationship, were they? No. They were about to have sex and this might be the only time in her life when she felt this way—out of control, trembling with anticipation for a man. It had never happened before. Who was to say that it would ever happen again?

If he thought she was easy, then so be it. She wasn't and

never had been. The most she could be accused of would be greed. Greed to taste what he had to offer.

Besides, within a couple of weeks she would walk away and never lay eyes on him again. His opinion of her wouldn't matter.

She was guiltily aware of a certain amount of double standards. She had been free to express her negative opinions of *him* and yet she was uncomfortably aware that he was now more than entitled to negative opinions of *her*—and she didn't care for it.

'I'm not having a change of mind,' she denied. 'My feet are sandy.'

'We can have a shower together…'

Leandro dealt her a slashing, sexy smile that made her toes curl.

'And I'm glad you're not having a change of mind…'

'I don't suppose it matters one way or the other, but I'm not…this person…'

Leandro raked his fingers through his hair and looked at her. 'You needn't have this conversation if you don't want to…'

Did he want to become embroiled in her anxieties? Was that what this was about? Absolutely not. And yet, despite what his mind was telling him, he found himself moving towards the bed, sitting on it, facing her. Her legs were crossed and her back was ramrod-straight. Every pore and muscle breathed nervous tension.

'Does my approval matter?' he asked with curiosity.

'Of course not!' Emily scoffed, blushing.

'How you choose to conduct yourself isn't my concern.'

'I realise that, Leandro, but I wouldn't want you to think… I know you've had a high opinion of me workwise…'

'But we're not talking about work here, are we?' He

gently pushed her back onto the pillows—to hell with the sand on their feet. 'I like the dress, by the way. Have I mentioned that?' He delicately slipped one strap off her shoulder and nibbled the soft skin there.

Emily felt as though a switch had been turned on inside her. The breath caught in her throat. Thinking clearly became an impossible task and she sighed as he continued to lick a delicate trail along her shoulder.

'This dress wasn't made for a bra…'

Her eyelids quivered as he disposed of it, shifting her so that he could unhook it from behind and then allowing her to wriggle free of it whilst keeping the dress intact.

He was mesmerised by the outline of her small breasts pushing against the slippery fabric. Just imagining what they would feel like in his big hands, what they would *taste* like, almost made him groan aloud.

He propped himself up on one elbow and gazed at her averted profile, her face tilted up, her eyes closed and her mouth parted.

'Take your clothes off for me…' he whispered huskily, and Emily turned to look at him.

Desire blazed in her eyes. Part of her couldn't believe she was doing this. Another part revelled in the freedom of being turned on without even having to work at it. She was so wet between her legs that her underwear was uncomfortable. It was shocking and intensely exciting at the same time.

'Don't tell me you're shy…?'

'Of course…er…of course not…' She laughed nervously and sat up so that she could free herself of the dress. His eyes were pinned to her. It was heady, knowing that he was watching—watching as she reached down to grasp the dress so that she could pull it over her head.

Her breasts bobbed, tiny and utterly tantalising, and Leandro couldn't resist. He pinned her to the bed and she gasped as his mouth sought and found one pert nipple, licking and sucking until she was tingling all over, unable to contain her whimpers of pleasure.

She couldn't keep still. Her fingers curled into his dark hair and she wanted his mouth everywhere. He moved from one nipple to the other and she squirmed and panted, took his hand so that she could guide it to the breast he wasn't suckling.

He was still in his clothes! And she was strangely too shy to take charge of undressing him. The hardness of his erection pressing against her was both thrilling and scary. She wanted to touch it but was afraid to. He felt absolutely massive!

He reared up so that he could yank his tee shirt over his head and then, moving to stand at the side of the bed, relieved himself of his trousers and underwear. She found herself sneaking a surreptitious glance at him.

She held her breath and tried not to gape as his nakedness captured every atom of her attention.

Even seeing him in his swimming trunks on the beach, barefoot and bare-chested, had not prepared her for the impact he had on all her senses.

Legs planted squarely on the ground, he watched her with amusement as she stared…and stared…and stared.

When he reached down to touch himself she nearly fainted.

She had tried to splutter out her guilty excuses along the lines of *not being that kind of girl*…but if Leandro had had any doubts on that score they were put to rest now, by her genuine reaction to seeing him standing in front of her in all his naked glory.

She was bright red, and as fast as her hungry eyes skittered away from the sight of him it seemed that they were compelled to return to looking at the very thing that was sending her into such heated confusion. She might have been a teenager in the presence of her very first lover.

'Enjoying the sight?' He grinned wickedly and watched her go an even deeper shade of pink.

'I…I'm not…'

'I get it.' He joined her on the bed and rolled her to face him so that they were looking at each other, their bodies pressed against one another. 'You're not the kind of girl who would have a sordid, short-lived liaison with a man whilst wearing an engagement ring on her finger because she's about to be married to someone else. Admittedly, though, there *is* no engagement ring…'

Because, he thought, love and romance were not part of the package deal. He eased off her underwear and his hand brushed the soft downy hair between her legs. He felt her wetness and gritted his teeth in an attempt to control his wayward libido.

'No,' Emily said breathlessly, 'I'm not.' *And yet she was…*

She moaned softly as he nudged apart her legs to insert his thigh between them, moving it slowly but insistently and sending currents of raging excitement through her.

'My perfect secretary…' he nuzzled her neck and covered one breast with his hand, massaging it while rubbing her stiffened nipple with his thumb '…has revealed complexities I would never have guessed at. Or maybe I would…'

Emily gave up all attempts to have a conversation. There was too much going on with her body. Too many sensations taking over. Everywhere throbbed—from her breasts to the damp patch between her legs, which he was teasing to the point of no return. She eased back and reached down to touch him, to hold him.

'You have to…stop…' she gasped '…doing that…'

'Doing what?' He removed his thigh and instead cupped her with his hand, and this time the rhythmic motion was even more devastating to her senses. 'This?'

'I'll… I won't be able to…hold back…' She could barely manage to speak!

'Good,' Leandro said with silky smoothness, enjoying her open, transparent reaction to what he was doing. In fact delighting in it in a way he couldn't remember having done with any other woman before. 'I'll enjoy watching you unable to hold back…'

He covered her mouth with his and kissed her with drugging intensity. All the time his hand was moving between her legs, and his fingers playing with the sensitised bud of her swollen clitoris was shockingly pleasurable.

She felt abandoned—wild, reckless and utterly liberated. For the first time she was a woman freed of all inhibition, able to enjoy her body and what was being done to it.

What crazy fool had ever suggested that love had to be part of the deal when it came to sex?

Maybe that was where she had gone wrong in the past. Getting to know the guys she had been dating, wishing herself in love, hoping that lust would naturally follow… Somehow it had never crossed her mind that she could just fancy a guy so much that he could drive her crazy with desire.

Least of all would she have figured on the guy in question being Leandro!

There was no embarrassment when she was tipped over the edge and rocked by wave after wave of orgasm. She flung her head back on a deep moan of sheer thrilling pleasure and allowed herself to be carried away.

It didn't matter that he was watching her in this most private of moments.

She arched back, shuddering as she came, and his mouth clamping to her nipple at that very instant was wildly, inconceivably erotic.

She looked at him shyly from under her lashes as her body slowly drifted back to Planet Earth.

With the speed of quicksilver it flashed through her mind that she couldn't have had more dreamily perfect sex in a more dreamily perfect setting.

'You *do* realise I'm not nearly finished with you...?'

'I do realise that,' Emily said gravely, and then, more daringly, 'And I hope you realise that *I* might not be finished with *you...*'

'I like the sound of that.' He sprawled back, inviting her to do whatever she wanted with him.

The man, she thought as she looked at him with openly appreciative eyes, was sexy beyond belief. No wonder women flocked around him like bees to honey.

She straddled him in one easy movement and Leandro delighted in her slimness, in the compact grace of her body, in the smallness of her neat breasts, still wet from where he had been licking them. She had caught the sun, and the bits of her that hadn't been exposed to it were pale and inviting.

He was rapidly coming to the conclusion that there were several things he disliked about the bodies of the women he had dated in the past. Not only the fact that all their body hair had been waxed into non-existence but also that their fullness, their overt voluptuousness, now seemed tacky and overdone. And they all seemed to have had an unhealthy predilection for acquiring all-over tans. He liked those pale lines on her—liked the way the rosiness of her disproportionately big nipples stood out...

He reached up to touch her breasts and she slapped his hands away. 'No,' she said firmly. 'No touching... I want to pleasure you now...'

'I get a ridiculous amount of pleasure from touching...'

Emily laughed. She might have been on some kind of drug, so heady did she feel.

She bent down to kiss him and her long hair fell in a silky canopy around their faces. His lips were hot and hungry and she smiled against his mouth because, strangely, she felt all-powerful. This unbelievably sexy man, *her boss,* was so turned on by her that he could scarcely control himself. His erection was an insistent rod of steel against her. He was so big that she wondered how on earth she would be able to accommodate him. And just thinking about that made her even wetter than she already was.

Her breasts brushed against his chest, setting off a series of chain reactions that were gloriously titillating. She had had no idea that her nipples were that sensitive.

She straightened and then wriggled herself so that she was sitting on his thighs and could hold him in her hand.

'Now it's my turn to watch,' she said.

She pushed her tangled hair away from her face impatiently. Squatting on him, her legs on either side, she made sure that as she stroked him his hardness also rubbed against her. His lazy, drowsy eyes regarded her with amusement.

He was anything but shy. He was a man who was completely comfortable in his own skin, she realised. Indeed, he was a man who was completely comfortable in the person he was.

It was why, she now knew, he could afford the luxury of romance. It was why he believed in marriage. It was why he thought that there was the right person out there for him.

Whereas *she*...

She breathed in deeply and slammed the door shut on the person she was—the person she had never expected to be once upon a time.

Leandro stilled her hand. Had he missed something? For a second he could have sworn that he had lost her, and yet now, as she gazed down at him with a half-smile that would have driven any man crazy, she was as she had been before.

'You…have…to stop…'

'What do you mean?'

'I mean a baby is not something I want…'

Emily nodded, understanding.

Her body was on fire, already missing its closeness to his, as he did what he had to do, fetching a condom from his wallet and putting it on with hands that were, she noticed, not completely steady.

'I don't take chances,' he grunted.

'And I can think of nothing worse,' Emily agreed with heartfelt sincerity.

Leandro was suddenly, fleetingly jealous of the guy she was destined to marry—even if it was to be a marriage of convenience. 'Sex with another guy when you're engaged is one thing…but a baby would be quite a different matter…'

'Catastrophic.' She pulled him towards her. 'Now, stop talking,' she commanded, 'and remember what I said about not being through with you…'

'I remember.' Leandro grinned with wicked pleasure. 'Take charge. I'm completely at your mercy…'

At her sweet, *sweet* mercy.

He loved everything she did to him. He loved the way she lathered him with kisses. He loved the way she teased him with her tongue. He loved the way her hair brushed like silk against his chest when she was down there, sucking and licking and sending him to another planet.

And, boy, he loved her enthusiasm. This wasn't lovemaking as an art form. She wasn't out to impress him with her inventiveness or her clever techniques.

She wanted him, and she wanted to enjoy him, and she wanted him to enjoy her. Simple as that.

When she sat on him and began rocking he could no longer restrain himself. If he didn't control the pace then he knew that the unthinkable would happen. He wouldn't be able to hold off. He would come within seconds, like a horny teenager with no finesse and even less experience.

He rolled her beneath him and took charge, moving into her and thrusting deep, rearing up to watch her face as she responded to every thrust, her legs wrapped around his back.

Still maintaining his rhythm, he bent and covered her mouth with his. His tongue mirrored what his hardness was doing, thrusting and enjoying her slick wetness.

As he moved faster and deeper he rose up, supporting himself with his hands flat on either side of her. He seemed to take in every single little detail of her. The shiny golden softness of her face, the length of her lashes, the little mole just above her right eyebrow, the bleached blondeness of her hair spread across the pillow, the scattering of freckles on her collarbone, the tan lines from where her swimsuit had been…

He came on an explosion of sensation that drove every thought out of his head. From a long way away he heard her cry out with satisfaction and it mirrored his own.

They were damp with perspiration, and as he collapsed on her their bodies seemed to stick together. He hadn't put the air-conditioning on and the overhead fan was inadequate when it came to cooling them down. It crossed his mind that *nothing* would have been adequate at cooling them down. They could have made love on an iceberg in the Arctic and they would still have been as hot as they were now.

'Did the Earth move for you too?' he asked huskily, and Emily nodded with a smile.

That was the understatement of the decade. The Earth had done more than just move! It had swivelled, spun in circles and done several loop-the-loops...

So *this* was what it felt like to be fired up with passion! Now she knew.

'I want to hear you say it,' he breathed, coiling his fingers into her hair and scattering delicate kisses on her mouth until she could feel her body getting fired up all over again.

'I...yes...the Earth moved for me too,' she breathed. 'I mean, I've never...'

'Never what...?'

'I've never...' She traced her finger along his chest, circled his flat brown nipple and watched it tighten at her touch. 'Never felt like that before with a guy...'

'And there have been lots...?'

Since when did he care how many lovers a woman had had before him? Insecure was something he most certainly was *not*, and yet now he wished he hadn't asked the question, because he didn't want to hear that he was just one in a long line of notches on her bedpost.

'No.' She laughed and brushed aside his question, because she didn't want to think about how many women there had been in *his* life. 'I'm not... I've never really fooled around...'

'You should learn from your past—not allow it to influence your present and your future. Your father may have been a monster but he doesn't represent the entire male sex...'

'I don't want to talk about that,' Emily said quickly.

It was a timely reminder of just how vastly different their worlds were. It was easy to simplify situations when you were speaking as a spectator to someone else's world. Not only was she a prisoner of her own learning curve but she also had to remember where she was now—about to be married and with no room for her thoughts to be muddled by a man who had been born with a silver spoon in his mouth.

'Then let's talk about what happens next...'

CHAPTER EIGHT

EMILY SHIELDED HER eyes against the glare of the sun and stared out at a picture postcard scene.

Overhead, the fronds of a palm tree blew lazily in the breeze and provided some welcome shade. If she looked up she would see the blue, cloudless sky, filtered through the branches of the tree. Now, looking outwards, her vista was one of the sea—bold turquoise gradually turning to a darker greeny-blue and then finally to midnight-blue where it was just a sharp line against the sky.

The sand was the consistency of caster sugar and almost the same colour. To her right, the little boat which had brought them here bobbed on the water. And in the distance Leandro was carelessly heading out towards the horizon, cutting a clean line through the calm water. He had no fear of all the things that panicked her when she thought about swimming beyond where she could touch the sea bed. Sharks…giant stingrays…barracuda… Various other unknown but deadly sea creatures waiting to pounce on the unwary swimmer.

He was completely naked. When he emerged from the sea she would feast her eyes on his gloriously masculine body and appreciate every line, every contour, every ripple of muscle. She would watch, fascinated, as he hardened for her. It amazed her just how much she turned him on.

She, likewise, was completely naked on a giant beach towel. They could afford to be here—gloriously naked—because the island was just an isolated dot. Sand, palm trees, flowering wild plants and accessible only by boat. They were the only two people on it, and when they had moored two hours earlier it had taken them under half an hour to walk its entire circumference.

Bliss.

Twenty minutes of walking and then making love in the open air—because *this* was what happened next.

They became lovers.

Just for a moment in time they agreed to give in to the crazy passion that had overwhelmed them. Why not? They were here and they fancied one another.

He hadn't asked her how it was that she could do what she was doing—making love to him with abandon—while counting down the days to her wedding. She hadn't stopped agonising over what his opinion of her would be, but she had acquired a skill for shoving it to the back of her mind. It was a skill she had been called upon to utilise many times over the past four days, during which they had made love like starstruck teenagers.

She had no inhibitions when she was with him. He had taken them all away from her and replaced them with a greedy craving that knew no limits. He didn't have to tell her where to touch him. She just seemed to know.

She watched, smiling, as he began swimming back towards shore, his strokes even and certain, his body becoming more and more defined the closer he got.

Her breath caught in her throat when, after a few minutes, he stood up and raked his fingers through his wet dark hair.

Quite simply put, the man was beyond beautiful, and she never tired of looking at him.

Eyes firmly fixed on her rapt face, even though he couldn't decipher the expression, Leandro lightly held himself and began walking slowly towards her.

He had cooled down after their earlier bout of lovemaking and now he was ready and raring for more. He could feel himself hardening in his hand, and by the time he was standing next to the towel, gazing down at her glorious body, he was rigid.

'Now look at what you've done...' He grinned, and then inhaled sharply as she sat up and took him in her mouth.

His hand behind her head, he stood completely still as she sucked and licked and teased his massive erection until he was groaning aloud and wondering if he should bother to try and control the orgasm that was hurtling towards him.

Never in his life had any woman been able to get him fired up to this extent.

Reluctantly he tugged her away and took a few seconds, trying to regain some kind of control over his body.

'You're a witch.'

He lay down next to her and drew her to him so that they were both on their sides, facing one another, their bodies fused. He nudged open her legs and felt her wetness against his thigh.

He could never have foreseen this. He could never in a million years have predicted that he and his secretary would end up in bed together. But now that they had he couldn't quite understand how it had not happened sooner.

Making love to her felt like the most natural thing in the world.

He kissed her—a long, lazy kiss—taking his time. He moved from her lips to her neck and she arched back as he nibbled the tender skin, targeting just that area by her ear where he knew she loved to be kissed.

The thrust of her breasts proved too tempting, and he

moved downwards to feast on one swollen nipple until she was whimpering and twisting underneath him.

She tasted good and he continued suckling, drawing the nipple into his mouth while he teased the rosebud tip of the other between his fingers.

'You're hot…' Barely shifting, he reached into the cooler they had brought with them, dislodged the lid and fumbled until he had an ice cube in his hand. 'You need cooling down. At least, these tender little nipples of yours do…'

He propped himself on his elbow and rolled the ice cube over the tip of her nipple, then circled it over her breast until she was moaning and giggling at the same time.

'Now, tell me that doesn't feel better…cooler…' He tossed the ice cube aside and continued his ministrations, licking and teasing the stiffened buds and then covering her breasts with kisses, heading south along the flat planes of her stomach.

He dipped his tongue into the indentation of her belly button and smiled as she inhaled sharply.

Her body responded to his each and every touch with exquisite immediacy. He felt as though she was a woman being touched for the first time, and in a way she was. She was inexperienced. Her past two boyfriends had failed to satisfy her. And hearing that had turned him on in ways he could hardly define.

He had made it his mission to do just the opposite—to turn her on to the point where she couldn't keep her hands off him, where she couldn't be in his radius without wanting him.

It was a two-way street, because he couldn't see her without touching her, couldn't keep his hands off her, and couldn't be bothered to try even when they were out in public.

He trailed his tongue lower, taking his time to explore

the satiny smooth skin of her belly, and then he gently parted her legs with his hand, preparing the way for what he would do next. Taste her. Feel her shift restlessly under him. Hear her soft little whimpers of delight.

She tasted of the warmth of the sun, the saltiness of the sea. He burrowed between her legs, licking and exploring every inch of her soft femininity with his tongue. She was damp and slippery and he loved the way she wrapped her legs over him and kept her hands firmly at her sides, fists clenched, every muscle in her body tuned in to what he was doing to her.

It was as if she were concentrating, focusing with her whole body on what was being done to it, with no sensation being taken for granted.

He physically ached from the constraint of not doing what his body was screaming to do—which was to come in her, hard and fast, until he was satisfied.

In the past, however much he'd been turned on by a woman, he had always been able to break things off in the event of an emergency. His mobile phone had always been switched on. The demands of work, even in the throes of passion, had always come first.

With Emily, it was different. He switched off his mobile phone. For hours on end. He was irritated when he got a call that interrupted time spent with her.

He felt her body begin to stiffen as wave upon wave of pleasure washed over her, threatening to take her over the edge.

Reluctantly, he raised himself to kiss her.

'I didn't want you to stop,' she complained, returning his kiss with little fluttery kisses of her own.

'I know. Nor did I. Have I ever told you how delicious you taste down there?'

Emily grinned, her eyes slumberous with a passion waiting to be sated. She wished she could hold this moment for ever—bottle it, perhaps, preserve it in some way so that it could remain intact.

'You may have...'

'I can think of a thousand things I'd like to eat off your body... Not that I imagine I would be able to exert sufficient self-control to do it...'

Emily's mind took flight at that. She watched as he reached across to the pile of clothes next to them, fumbling until he found protection, and all the while she could picture him licking ice cream from her stomach, honey from her nipples, all manner of sweet things from everywhere, until she was driven wild.

She pictured herself doing the same to him.

She was waiting, ready for him as he inserted himself inside her, big and powerful and filling every inch of her.

Her fingers dug into his shoulders as he began to move, thrusting deeper and deeper so that the beach towel was rucked underneath them. Eyes closed, she blindly sought his mouth and found it, and then she lost herself in a never-ending kiss as he continued to bring her faster and faster towards her climax.

When she came, she flung her head back and held her breath, before crying out as her orgasm took over her body, banishing all thought and carrying her away to another place completely.

He was holding her tightly, timing his own climax, holding off before allowing himself to let go, feeling her every reaction and responding to each one with unerring instinct.

They came as one and he groaned and stiffened as he spilled his seed into the condom, wishing with shocking unexpectedness that he could feel her without the protective sheath dulling the sensation.

'I'm hot,' she said sleepily as he disposed of the used

condom and settled down on the towel with his arms around her, their bodies spent.

'Perhaps we should give it a few minutes before we resume activity,' he murmured, grinning. 'I may be super-human when it comes to making love, but even I have my limits…'

'I didn't mean I was hot *for you*. I meant that I was… *hot*…'

'A man's ego could be crushed…'

He kissed the side of her mouth and then decided to linger a little longer there. And holding her breast would, he decided, feel pretty good too. So small and delightfully soft.

'Let's go for a dip,' he suggested. 'Then lunch. I've had your favourite prepared.'

'You don't know what my favourite is…'

'Of course I do! Sandwiches…brown bread…with ham…all fat cut off…lettuce and tomato, mayonnaise, no mustard. Or chicken salad…no celery… Fried fish is also on the menu…with ketchup and lots of it…'

'How on earth do you know that?'

But she knew how he did. They did a lot of talking, and sometimes about the most inconsequential of things. He had compiled a random set of facts about her just as she had about him.

She felt a stirring of unease blow over her like a cold breeze. She reminded herself that this was just time out— an adventure before she resumed the reality of her life back in England.

'I seem to know a lot about you, my dear secretary. Maybe it's been a process of osmosis over the many months you've worked for me…'

He heaved himself up and extended his hand, inviting her to take it, which she did.

His eyes roamed appreciatively over her naked body as

she stood up, long and slender, with the grace of a ballet dancer. It was a body that should never have been concealed beneath dreary work clothes and prim, unappealing suits.

'I think your pubic hair is going lighter in the sun,' he commented.

Emily grinned and reddened. His fingers were curled into hers and it felt...comfortable.

'I could say the same about you,' she retorted, half running and dragging him along.

'You couldn't.' He spun her round, held her tight and devoured her mouth in a long, leisurely kiss. 'I'm brown and my hair everywhere is dark. Dark enough to defy all attempts by the sun to lighten it. What colour hair does the fiancé have?'

He hadn't meant to ask that. In fact he had decided to avoid all mention of her fiancé. As far as he was concerned, as long as they were out here, the man didn't exist. He had no idea if she spoke to him daily or not at all.

So how was it that the question had slipped out so easily? And, now that it had, how did it make sense that he was eagerly waiting for the answer? When he couldn't care less?

'Fair.' She turned away, not wanting to prolong any conversation on the subject of Oliver.

She had spoken to him a couple of times since they had arrived on the island. Now and again her decision to marry him, for reasons that had made perfect sense before she had become involved with Leandro, jarred on her conscience, no longer seemed quite so clear cut.

She hit the water and dismissed her misgivings by diving in, enjoying the cool against her skin after the heat. She swam out and continued swimming, further than she would normally have done, and only spluttered to a stop when she felt Leandro's arms around her.

'So you don't want to talk about him?' he heard himself say.

They could both still touch the sand but the water was past their waists.

'No, I don't.'

She looked away from him but he caught her face in his hand.

'Why not?'

'Because… You know why, Leandro…'

'Because you don't want to be reminded that I'm your dirty little secret?'

'No!'

'What would you say if I told you that that's how I feel?'

'I wouldn't believe you.' Her heart was beating wildly. 'I mean, we both know that this is just a temporary thing…' And yet why did she wince when she uttered those words which were nothing less than the truth?

Their eyes tangled and he released her. 'Swim back to shore, Emily. I need to head out further.'

'Okay.'

Leandro scowled. She was desperate to get rid of him—desperate to avoid any conversation that might compromise her sense of morality, which was kept conveniently under wraps while she slept with him here but which would, without a shadow of doubt, regain the high ground the second the plane touched down at Heathrow in a matter of a few scant days.

He struck out with the restless feeling that their conversation was not over, and when he finally turned around to head back to the beach, after twenty minutes of vigorous swimming, he had come to the decision that he wasn't going to let it rest.

It irked him further to find that she was in her swimsuit waiting for him, sunglasses in place, hat on, book in hand.

'I thought we could have some lunch now.' Emily licked her lips nervously and laid the book down on the towel next to her.

'Is that why you decided to don the swimsuit?' Leandro reached for his towel, roughly dried himself and then slung the towel loosely round his waist. 'Because you thought that it was time for lunch?'

He sat down, positioning himself neatly in front of the cooler so that she couldn't busy herself taking food out and pouring drinks when they still had a conversation to finish.

'We only have a couple more days left here,' he said.

'I know.' Emily resigned herself to a conversation she wasn't sure she wanted. 'I think we've accomplished everything that we...er...set out to do.'

'I'm surprised you still include yourself in this project when you'll be quitting pretty much as soon as we return to London.'

'I said that I'd stay to effect a hand-over with my replacement and I will.'

Leandro ignored her pedestrian foray into a discussion about work. He wasn't in the mood.

Instead he looked at her in silence for such a long time that she eventually broke eye contact and stared out to sea.

'So, are we going to talk about what's happening between us?'

Leandro's body language mirrored hers, but he was one hundred per cent focused on *her*, even though he, too, was staring out to sea. He could feel her next to him and was alert to every shift in her position. He was aware of her tension, and of her reluctance to be drawn into talking about what he intended to talk about.

Emily shrugged and he fought down a wave of intense

irritation. For some reason he was on the back foot and it annoyed the hell out of him. When it came to women it was not in him to pursue. But this felt like pursuit. He told himself that of course it wasn't. It was the purely under-standable reaction of a man facing the demise of a sexual relationship which he knew neither he nor his lover really wanted to end. He wasn't chasing. He was expressing a natural curiosity as to what happened next.

'I don't see the point,' she mumbled at last.

He turned to her, and although he was perfectly still there was a savage intensity to his voice that made her stiffen.

'Can you honestly tell me that you want what we have to end when we return to London?'

'It doesn't matter whether I want it to end or not.'

'I want you to look at me when I'm talking to you.'

Emily reluctantly shifted so that she was facing him.

'And I want to see your eyes.'

He reached across and whipped off her sunglasses so that she immediately felt vulnerable and unprotected.

More than anything else she wished that he would just drop this—wished that they could return to the physical-ity that was as addictive as a drug. She didn't want to think about whether she wanted this to continue or not when they returned to London because as far as she was concerned there was no option. It would have to end—like it or not. For reasons that were not in her control.

'So talk to me,' he commanded roughly. 'Tell me how it is that you can square this with your conscience—marry another man when you still burn for me.'

'I…'

'Yes?'

'I told you… I'm not romantic like…like all those other women you've gone out with…'

'I get it. You had a bloody awful learning curve when you were young. But don't tell me that you would sacrifice your life on the back of *that*.'

'I wouldn't be sacrificing my life, Leandro.'

'You would be making a foolish choice, and once that choice has been made you will find yourself nailed to it and unable to break free if you should ever want to.'

'There *is* such a thing as divorce...'

'I don't believe I'm hearing this.'

'And I don't believe that we're having this conversation!' Emily cried. 'You should be thankful that I'm not one of those clingy women who wants to latch onto you and never let go! You should be glad that you don't have to deal with mopping up my tears because you want to get rid of me and I won't let you!'

'I should be, shouldn't I...? And yet all I can do is feel pity for a woman who's about to commit herself to a loveless marriage, for reasons best known to her, with the opt out clause of divorce if it proves to be the disaster it undoubtedly will...'

He swivelled round and began offloading the cooler, but his appetite was non-existent.

'I *knew* you would think less of me if we became...became...if we slept together!'

'You're right. I have no admiration for what you're doing.'

'There's a lot you don't know.'

'Then why don't you try telling me?'

Silence thickened between them.

'Oh, I see. None of my business.'

'What do you want from me?'

'Honest answer?' He paused and looked her directly in the eye. 'I want you to have the courage to admit that it would be a mistake to marry a man when you're clearly hot for another one.'

'It's not all about sex.'

'You want me. That's not going to go away when we return to London and you step back into your prim little work suits...'

'That's what this is all about, isn't it?' Agitated, Emily sprang to her feet and spun round to stare down at him. 'You're not ready for this to end because *you* always dictate the terms of your relationships, don't you?'

'That's *not* what this is about!' But Leandro had the grace to flush darkly.

'Of course it is!' She began walking towards the sea but then, as though compelled, she turned back to glare at him, her arms folded, her body rigid with tension.

This was not a place meant for arguing. It was too breathtakingly beautiful. And she didn't want to argue. In fact she didn't even want to think about the fact that Paradise would only be theirs for a few more short days.

'You go out with women and when you tire of them you move on. You're annoyed because you're not ready to move on quite yet!'

'I'm frustrated because I see a woman on the verge of throwing her life away...'

'And, like any decent knight in shining armour, you want to save me from my fate? Is that it? You just want to set me on the right path? You're being one hundred per cent altruistic with no hidden agenda at all...?'

'My agenda is anything but hidden,' Leandro drawled, and the hot intensity of his dark eyes made the blood rush to her face. 'Can you honestly tell me that you want this to end the second we step foot on British soil? Can you honestly tell me that that's even possible?'

'Of course it is. We're just having a... This is just a...a... *dalliance*...'

Leandro looked at her in silence for a long time. Finally he shrugged. 'So be it.'

He began unpacking the picnic hamper, laying things out on the rug which had been provided by the hotel. As always, they had prepared a feast. There was chilled wine, but after a brief hesitation he ignored that and went for the bottled water instead.

'So be it?'

The conversation felt as though it had been killed off ahead of schedule. Was that it? A shrug of the shoulders and onward bound?

'I think it's time we ate, and then we'll head back to the island.'

He tucked into one of the sandwiches and poured himself some water. He wasn't looking at her, but out of the corner of his eye he could see her wary stance, the tense set of her shoulders, the stubborn line of her full mouth.

'Sure.'

'And you can consider your contract with my company terminated as from the second we get back to the UK.'

'What—what are you talking about?' Emily stammered. She sat down on the rug, legs crossed, and stared at the array of food—none of which she felt like eating.

'I'm saying that there will be no need for you to work out the remainder of your notice. You will be free to go as soon as we are off this island. And for the rest of the time that we're here we'll focus exclusively on what we came here to do. Work.'

'And all this just because I won't do as you say?'

When she stared at the sandwiches and fruit laid out in front of her she saw instead a progression of empty, Leandro-less days stretching out as far as the eye could see.

She blinked the disturbing vision away. She was set on a certain course and there was no getting off it. And it would be great not having to work out her notice. Wouldn't it? She would be free to get on with the rest of her life, putting in place the necessary things that had to be done…

'We can… I realise you don't understand why I'm doing what I'm doing, why I'm going ahead with… Well, things are never neatly explained away…' She heard herself fumbling with her words, tripping over excuses she couldn't give him, and she flushed at the cynical twist of his mouth.

'I mean…' She reached out, dry-mouthed, and placed her hand on his.

A world without Leandro felt, right now and right here, like a very bleak and empty world. But she knew that that wouldn't last. She was caught up in a bubble where normal reactions and day-to-day reality were suspended. The second she was back on home ground what she felt would vanish like mist on a summer's day, but for now why couldn't she just reach out and bring him back to her, back to the place where they were as one…?

Whatever he had said, and however disappointed he claimed to be with the choices she was making, surely what they had was so strong that he would not be able to resist the temptation to take this through at least until they left the island? Surely she wasn't alone in wanting that?

'I really don't think so…'

Leandro politely removed her hand and Emily licked her lips and stared at him, mortified at the rejection.

'We're attracted to one another,' she said shakily. 'You said so yourself…'

'We are… But I've come to the conclusion that I'm no longer willing to take what's on offer—not with the baggage involved…'

He had barely tasted what he had eaten. He crumpled the

foil in which the sandwich had been wrapped and tossed it into the open cooler, then looked at her coolly.

'For me, this hasn't run its course. But I have no intention of following it through for a couple more days until you go running back to your cuckolded fiancé...'

It would have been impossible for Emily to have gone any redder.

'So you're giving me an ultimatum? Leave Oliver or else things go back to how they were before we came here...?'

She blinked back tears of hurt and rejection. She should be angry with him for his double standards, for his wanting her to adapt her whole life to suit him when he would not have done likewise for her.

'Throw in my marriage for the sake of a few weeks of fun with you...?'

'Who said anything about it lasting a few weeks? Could be less...could be more...'

'And I'm honestly supposed to sacrifice my future for "could be less...could be more..."?'

'If you could convince me that this future of yours wasn't worth sacrificing then we wouldn't be having this conversation now. In fact I'm presuming that if this future of yours was that meaningful we wouldn't have ended up in bed in the first place...'

He stood up and without the slightest hint of embarrassment flung the towel aside and put on the swimming trunks which he had discarded the minute they had reached the island.

Without looking at him, Emily began clearing away the remains of what they had eaten. Most of it was left and she hoped that the chef wouldn't be upset. The fact was that she couldn't have had another bite if her life had depended on it.

She didn't know what else to say. He had withdrawn

from her, and that was evident in his cool politeness as they packed their things away in silence and the boat went back to the main island, likewise in silence.

Her sporadic attempts at conversation were met with a detachment that chilled her to the bone.

So this was what it felt like, she thought with despair. This was what love felt like. She had fancied herself in complete control of the situation and had thrown herself wholeheartedly into an affair on the assumption that snatching a couple of weeks of undiluted happiness would have no lasting consequences. She wasn't made for falling in love and yet it had ambushed her from behind. Life without Leandro was like staring down the barrel of a gun.

She sat on her hands because she was so tempted to reach out and touch him. When had all her defence mechanisms fallen by the wayside? When had lust turned into love? She couldn't pinpoint a moment in time. She just knew that she would have to grab what was on offer and run with it or else live a life of regret, and she didn't think she had the strength to live with regret. It would not make a happy companion.

The minute they were back at the hotel, after the longest boat ride and Jeep drive in her entire life, he picked up some polite threads of conversation. She thought that it was purely to accommodate the fact that there were other people around them now—people who had cheerfully accepted the relationship between boss and secretary and would have been curious had they witnessed its breakdown first-hand.

But *she* was miserably aware of the change in him. The safety of the future she had planned now seemed as flimsy as a wisp of smoke. So much would have been sorted with this marriage, so many problems solved, and everything would have been fine had she had her heart intact. She would have entered into it as the business proposition both she and Oliver had agreed on.

Now she knew that any such business proposition was just not meant to be, and for a few seconds she was furious with Leandro for throwing everything out of kilter.

He had tossed her a carrot and it wasn't even a very good one. A few weeks—maybe longer, maybe not—of having fun in bed and then he would be off, in search of another playmate.

He promised nothing because he had nothing to give, and whilst she appreciated the honesty she resented the fact that in the end he could wield such power over her. She resented the fact that her ammunition had been so shockingly incomplete. She resented the love that was burning a hole through her.

He turned to her when they were briefly out of earshot of any of the attendant staff. 'Feel free to dine tonight in your room. I have things I need to catch up on and I shall probably be busy for the remainder of the day and this evening.'

He leaned against the wooden railing that skirted the dining area. Heavy bougainvillaea, abloom with bright red and orange flowers, shielded them from the sun and threw his handsome face into shadow. That said, she was still perfectly capable of making out the cold, set line of his jaw and the aloofness in his eyes.

Hesitantly she reached out and placed her hand on his arm. She didn't remove it when he looked at it and then back at her, his expression hard and unforgiving.

'You can look,' he drawled, 'but you have lost the right to touch.'

'No, I haven't.'

She looked him squarely in the face. Her voice was calm and controlled but her heart was beating like a jackhammer and her mouth was dry.

'Come again?' Leandro found that he was holding his breath, watching her face intently, barely able to move a muscle.

'You're right,' she said quietly. 'I can't marry Oliver. Not when this is happening between us. Safety might be appealing, but what we have is too strong to resist. So I'm going to call him as soon as I get to my room and tell him that the marriage is…off…'

CHAPTER NINE

EMILY STRETCHED OUT on the massive king-sized bed and did a slow visual tour of the bedroom.

This was her routine every time she stayed the night at his apartment. Sex, and a great deal of it, then a pleasantly fractured night's sleep during which one or the other might reach out blindly and their bodies would fuse, even though they might both be half asleep, and in the morning while he went downstairs to make them both a cup of coffee before the day began *this*...this visual tour of his bedroom. She was committing it to memory because, although it had been nearly five weeks since they had returned to the UK, she knew that she was living on borrowed time.

Having broken up with Oliver, she had given up on worrying. The problems her marriage to him would have solved were still there, but it was no longer in her to angst over them. The solution she had found had disappeared the day she had phoned her fiancé and told him that the wedding was off.

But what else could she have done? Love had bludgeoned her from behind and she had felt as though her options had been limited. Sleep with Leandro and break off her engagement—take, in other words, what was on offer or else endure a lifetime of bitter regret.

She knew that she was falling deeper and deeper in love

with him. She also knew that it was a feeling that was not reciprocated. She was his plaything. A different sort of plaything from the ones he had dated in the past, but still his plaything. He liked her well enough, and he enjoyed her company, but falling in love was certainly not what he was in the process of doing.

The word *love* never crossed his lips. That was an emotion reserved for the special woman he would eventually find and marry—because, as she had discovered, he really did believe that marriages could work out. You had to be realistic, he had said, and had shrugged with a smile, but love was not an impossible dream. What, he had asked her, would be the point of working, earning money, fulfilling ambitions small or great, if at the end of it you were too cynical, too bitter or too disillusioned to enjoy sharing the rewards with someone else?

Working for him, she would never have guessed it. She had written him off as someone else like her father—just another philandering man who didn't care how he treated women as long as he could get from them what he wanted. Another man who didn't give a damn about his discards.

She had discovered that he was nothing like her father. He occasionally spoke about his exes with affection, and if there had been a higher than average number of girlfriends in the past then, he had laughingly told her, it was because he was extremely cautious about getting too wrapped up with any one woman when he knew, in his heart, that she was not the one for him—not the one with whom he wanted to form a permanent relationship.

In fact, he had assured her, he was the consummate gentleman when it came to the fairer sex.

Emily would have laughed with outright derision at that a few weeks previously, but after digging a little deeper she had discovered that he kept in touch with a surprising number of his exes.

Two he had set up in their own businesses. He was godfather to the children of a few of them, and took his duties as godfather very seriously.

'It's the Latin American way,' he had told her smugly. 'We're big into families... When I eventually settle down I shall expect the lucky lady to agree with me that a nice round number like six is perfect when it comes to children...'

When he spoke like that she could feel something twist painfully inside her.

She assumed that 'the lucky lady' would be from his own country—a sexy, dark-haired beauty who was possibly a family friend and knew the way his world worked. Someone from the same elevated background.

She never asked what this woman would be like or where he might find her. She didn't want to have answers to those questions, and at any rate he would have been surprised had she asked. They were lovers with an understanding. She wasn't looking for anything else and so, like him, could enjoy their relationship without inconveniently wanting more.

And it helped that she no longer worked for him. He had pulled strings, despite her protests, and found her an equally well paid job at a law firm in the City.

The responsibilities were different, but she found that she enjoyed the work, enjoyed the variation in her tasks... enjoyed playing with the idea of possibly becoming a paralegal...

She knew that she should have objected to having him help her get another job. Pulling strings was not something of which she approved. But she needed the money. It was as simple as that. And he had swept aside her concerns by reminding her that she had been a brilliant employee, that Stern, Hodge and Smith should consider themselves lucky to have nabbed her…

All these thoughts were lazily swirling through her mind as she looked at the hand-crafted chest of drawers by the window, the fall of the curtains, the built-in wardrobes fashioned from the same smooth, blond and tan wood as the dressing table.

There was an original Picasso—a small, exquisite sketch—casually hanging over the chest of drawers, and more than anything else that was a constant reminder of how different their worlds were.

She glanced away as she heard the sound of him nearing the room and helplessly watched the door, waiting for him to nudge it open, already anticipating the little thrill of delight that would shoot through her the second she saw him. She hated this weakness in herself, this absolute powerlessness when it came to him, but she accepted it just as she accepted that after a lifetime of being in control, of always remaining on the sidelines, a spectator to any emotion that might suck her under, she was no longer in that position.

'You're up.'

Leandro looked at her with open male satisfaction— looked at the duvet which was making a poor attempt at covering her nakedness, looked at the spread of her blonde hair across the pillow and the way her blue eyes lazily drank him up, as shamelessly appreciative of his nudity as he was of hers.

Emily wound a strand of long hair around her finger and smiled. 'I was up when you left the bedroom.'

'Really?'

'I didn't want you to know because I wanted to see that cute little rear of yours as you walked out of the bedroom.

I didn't want you to be modest and hide it away from me under your dressing gown...'

'Modest? I feel you're thinking of the wrong guy...' He never failed to marvel that she could be like this...soft and sexy and teasing...nothing at all like his dim recollection of how she'd used to be when she worked for him.

He frowned and moved to place her coffee on the table next to the bed. 'You've never told me what the people you work with are like,' he said suddenly.

He eased himself next to her and reached behind to cover her peachy bottom with his hand, so that with very little pressure he could draw her towards him and feel the length of her nakedness pressed against his.

'You've told me,' he continued, nibbling her neck, then the side of her mouth, before drawing back and settling her into the crook of his arm, 'that you get along with them, but what does that mean? It's been a while since I went to see old Hodge. Can't really remember what kind of ship he's running there...'

'It's a tight one, Captain...' She traced his bare chest with her hand. 'Have I told you that I'm interested in maybe doing a bit more than just being a PA? I think I could really do well in law. I enjoy it. I enjoy the precision...'

Leandro grunted. He wasn't that interested in her future career as a hotshot corporate lawyer. 'I was thinking more along the lines of the people you work with. I wouldn't want to have set you up with a job where you're surrounded by bores...'

'Well, you can rest assured that they're all very interesting.'

'*All* of them? Is that possible?'

'It's a great environment, Leandro. I mean, it's different from your office. It's not nearly as big, and there's a much higher concentration of young people of similar educational background...'

It wasn't what Leandro wanted to hear. His scowl deepened. He couldn't quite see when his ridiculously powerful attraction to her was going to end, and if *he* felt that way—if she could hold *his* attention for that length of time—then wasn't it conceivable that other guys would be ogling her? It made perfect sense. And how long would it take her to realise that she could hitch up with someone there? Someone who would tempt her with the offer of a committed relationship...someone who would rival the now ex-fiancé when it came to safety?

Leandro, in a vague way, had always assumed that any love connection for him would come in the form of an Argentinian girl—someone who would understand what was expected of her, someone whose goal in life would be to have his children and run a smooth household...someone whose career would be *him*. And, of course, someone who wasn't after him for his money.

His mother had been the perfect wife to his dad. She had had a handful of children and had been proud to take care of her husband's needs. Was he old-fashioned in thinking that that would be the right sort of woman for him when the time came? As opposed to a career woman who imported nannies to look after her kids and fainted at the thought of staying at home? Or else an empty-headed beauty who would be willing to do whatever he wanted just so long as he kept pouring money into her hands? Someone who would jump ship should the money ever stop?

Emily Edison—secretary extraordinaire, sex bomb extraordinaire and now career woman in the ascendant—didn't fit the bill. So he was a little perplexed as to why the thought of other men looking at her bothered him. He wasn't a possessive man. Such feelings were entirely inappropriate when it came to mistresses.

'Is that a fact?' He straddled her and began lathering attention on her neck, her shoulders, her collarbone. 'And have any of these fun guys of a similar age made a pass at you yet?'

Emily looked at him with muted surprise. 'Are you jealous?'

'I don't do jealousy. I do curiosity.'

'Ah. Right…' She felt a twinge of disappointment but she understood completely. 'I haven't been there long enough to get into any kind of social life.'

'And furthermore you don't *need* a social life as you have me. You're also recovering from a broken engagement…'

Curiosity…irresistible, dangerous, compelling.

Had she *really* broken off with her fiancé? If there had been any doubt then it should have been laid to rest by the amount of time they spent in each other's company. Just like that she had kissed a sweet goodbye to the engagement that had propelled her into handing in her resignation.

But his curiosity had been challenging to shift. Was the guy just biding his time…waiting until what they had blew over?

Somehow the thought of that enraged Leandro, and he looked at her now, his mind playing between the equally unpleasant scenarios of several young men chasing her in her place of work or one young man waiting for her on the sidelines.

There was nothing he could do about an ardent following in her workplace, short of buying the company, sacking the entire lot and replacing them with elderly, happily married men.

A tempting thought, if only it were feasible.

But what of his ex-competition? Cheerfully dispatched

or still hovering in the background, nurturing hopes of a grand reunion? Red roses in his hand and engagement ring still in its box, ready to be whipped out once more at short notice?

He realised that he had wasted more time than he would ever have expected thinking about her ex.

He didn't even know what the guy looked like!

What was to stop him doing just a little background check? Maybe establishing whether the man was still on the scene or not....? Putting his mind to rest that she was his and his alone for the duration of their relationship.

He had never had a chauvinistic bone in his body—was in full agreement that women were entitled to the same rights as their male counterparts in the workplace—but...

He felt primitive with *her*.

It made no sense. He wasn't looking for anything beyond what she had cheerfully told him was on the table. She didn't believe in relationships, in any of the things most women believed in, and so she came to him with no strings attached and no expectations lingering in the background.

And yet, perversely, he was far more intent on reassuring himself that he possessed her utterly than he had ever been with any other woman.

The thought of her trying him on for size because her ex-fiancé didn't quite cut it on the physical front was abhorrent to him.

Worse was the notion that she might leave him and use everything she had experienced as a learning curve with which to re-energise her physical relationship with the ex.

Always presuming that the damned man was still on the scene!

It would take one call and he could put the whole thing into motion. Find out where the ex was...whether he was

out of the picture completely…what the man looked like…
what precisely he did for a living…

With one number dialled on his mobile he could be in
possession of facts which he knew should not concern him
and which were, essentially, none of his business.

'Everyone needs a social life, Leandro.'

It took him a few seconds to return to what they had
been talking about. 'Come again?'

'*You're* not my social life.'

Emily decided to get that perfectly straight, because
falling in love with him was one thing… It would be quite
another for him to get any inkling that he was the centre
of her universe. Pride would never allow her to give him
that privilege.

'You're telling me that you have after-work fun with
the young lawyers in the company? Drinks in those overpriced, over-stylised pubs that bear no resemblance to what
a real pub should look like?'

'I'm too busy finding my feet to have much time for that
at the moment,' Emily told him truthfully. 'But I expect
I shall in due course. It's a very sociable crowd of young
people who work there.'

'And what's happened to…? I forget his name… The
ex-fiancé…'

'Oliver.'

'That's it. Is he still on the scene?'

'He's a friend, first and foremost,' Emily said vaguely.
'We keep in touch.'

'Cosy.'

'*You* keep in touch with some of your ex-girlfriends…'

'I don't recall ever having been engaged to any of them.'

'What difference does that make?'

'None of my relationships ever went that far. If and when
I ever get to the point where I'm ready to commit and be-

come engaged to a woman, then I sure as hell wouldn't
be passing the time of day with her if it didn't work out.'

He leapt out of the bed, grabbing his mobile on the way.
'Where are you going?'

Sudden panic washed over Emily. Always on the alert
for signs of boredom setting in, she wondered whether this
random conversation about the great big world happening
outside their little bubble had reminded him that he was
still a single guy—still a guy looking for the right woman.
Had talk of broken engagements and near-miss weddings
turned him off the thrill of having a mistress? Had it sown
the pernicious seed of wanting more than just passing sex?

He had vanished out of the bedroom and she remained
frozen where she was. Part of her wanted to rush behind
him and demand to know what was going through his
head. The other part wanted no such thing—wanted just
to stay where she was and hope for the best, hope that things
weren't beginning to fall apart between them.

She breathed a long sigh of relief when he returned to
the bedroom five minutes later. 'Where did you go?' she
asked casually.

'Had to make a phone call.' He chucked the phone onto
the stack of discarded clothing on the ground and climbed
back into bed with her.

Job done. A single phone call. His man would set everything in motion and have whatever answers he needed
before the end of the day.

Leandro didn't like spying, and he certainly would never
tell her what he had done because there would be no point,
but his good mood had been restored. He had never cared
for unresolved issues.

'Now, where were we…?' He dealt her a slashing smile
and returned to kissing her, taking up where he had left
off and sliding into the soft response of her body as easily

and seamlessly as if there had been no awkward conversation between them.

Emily lay back and curled her fingers into his dark, tousled hair. When he touched her she couldn't think, and that was a pretty good place to be.

Her breasts were aching in anticipation of what he was going to do to them, the attention he was going to lavish there. She arched and then sighed as he took one pouting pink nipple into his mouth and began to suckle. He told her often and in great detail how much he loved her breasts, and why. Having spent a lifetime thinking that they were too small, she had learnt to offer them to him, knowing that they turned him on.

In fact the same could be said of her entire body. Was that part of the reason why she had been so susceptible to him? Why she had been unable to stop herself from falling in love with him? Because he had burrowed beneath her fortresses and found the person who had been hiding? The trusting, hopeful girl who had spent so long concealing herself behind a wall of ice?

Fat lot of good it would do her in the end, because he was not available for anything more than a fling, but Emily had learnt to cut short those thoughts when they appeared.

His mouth clamped to her nipple was bliss. He sucked hard, and as he sucked his tongue flicked over the stiffened bud, driving her crazy. She couldn't get enough. She touched the nipple he wasn't attending to, pinching it between her fingers, and he gently pushed her hand away so that he could cup it and play with it himself.

'You can touch yourself down there,' he broke away for a second to say, with a grin that notched up the heat level roaring through her body. 'Keep yourself nice and wet until I get there...'

As if to demonstrate exactly what he meant, he covered

her hand with his and positioned it neatly between her legs, then he slid it into her wetness, pausing only to glance over his shoulder, even more aroused as he watched her play with herself. He could hear the soft, slick sound of her wet fingers and he stifled a groan of pure lust.

He had to press down firmly on his erection to stop himself from being tempted to rush things so that he could hurry towards his own satisfaction.

He let her tease him with her hands and her mouth, but he had to pull back often, because she knew just how to arouse him, just how to tip him over the edge. It was as if she had complete control over his body. And whilst it was bloody marvellous on the one hand, on the other it did require a great deal of self-control and gritting of teeth to stop himself from coming prematurely.

He moved down to lick her stomach, squirming his tongue into the neat indentation of her belly button and enjoying her little whimpers of pleasure. Then he covered her hand with his and eased himself down along her body until he could breathe in the sweet, fragrant aroma of her womanhood.

He parted the shell-like lips and dipped his tongue in—just a quick flick, establishing intent. Then he blew softly, which had her almost completely melting and wriggling, so he stilled her with his hand even though he knew that she would be finding it difficult to keep still.

Her body burned for his. She twisted and he tapped her gently and told her to keep still,

'Or,' he drawled, 'I'll have to introduce a little light bondage... Would you like that?'

The image nearly sent her into meltdown. She nodded and blushed, and then met his eyes with hers and held his stare.

'You're turned on at the thought of it, aren't you, my darling?' Leandro grinned.

If he hadn't been so hot, and so in need of finishing what they had started, he would have hunted down something suitable to take their lovemaking down a slightly different road. But that, he decided, would have to wait. He literally wouldn't be able to hold out for the time it would take to find some strips of cloth…

In fact he could barely hold out long enough after he had licked and teased that swollen bud to equip himself with a condom, but equip himself he did.

Emily felt that her body would combust if he didn't fill her soon. He was so big, so thick, that when he entered her, her entire body was set alive, every nerve-ending satisfied.

But, as usual, he would do nothing until he had ensured protection. Even though she was now on the pill, and even though she had told him more than once that there was no need for him to wear a condom.

Even the pill, he had told her, could fail, and he wasn't going to be taking any chances…

More than anything else this told a story of its own. The guy who wanted a football team of kids would never take chances unless it was with a woman he truly cared about—a woman with whom he could envisage having those children.

Underneath the burning lust, how could he respect someone who had slept with him when she had been engaged to someone else? He had never, ever said anything to give her any reason to believe that contempt laced his feelings towards her, but deep down she harboured that nagging worry.

It was just something else she had conditioned herself to ignore—because what would be the point of analysing it? She closed her eyes and gasped with pleasure as he thrust deep into her, and then again, moving strong and hard and banishing her uncomfortable thoughts until sensation took over, spiralling and spilling over into wave upon wave of shuddering orgasm.

Their rhythms matched perfectly. Their bodies were so tuned in to one another that instinct guided them. When they came, they came together.

She felt his big body lose control and, as always, felt the heady sensation of absolute happiness that this man could do this to her and she could do the same for him.

Subsiding back to Planet Earth, Leandro almost missed the sound of his cell phone buzzing from where he had earlier chucked it.

Emily was fond of telling him that he had no respect for his possessions. He treated his expensive clothes as though they'd been bought cheap at a market and were disposable. He had a drawer full of smartphones, most of which had cracked screens. But Leandro found that her gentle nagging did not irritate him in the slightest. On the contrary, he rather enjoyed it—although he wasn't quite sure why.

'Your phone's ringing.'

Emily lay back and stretched and for a few seconds Leandro was driven to watch her, because the movement was so unconsciously graceful.

'I'm busy. I'll get it later.'

'What are you busy doing?'

'I'm busy looking at the woman in my bed.'

Emily blushed and savoured the appreciative gleam in his dark eyes. 'It could be important.'

'Not as important as watching you. Or...' he slid out of the bed, reached down and scooped her up in one easy movement '...as important as having a bath with you. It's fair to say that both those activities take precedence over some work-related issue that can be dealt with later...'

He enjoyed having baths with her. He liked the feel of her body when it was wet and slick with soapsuds. It reminded him of how she had felt in the sea…with his arms around her… Those last few days on the island after she had come to him had been mind-blowing. Occasionally he caught himself wondering whether he shouldn't engineer another spurious work-related trip out there just so that they could repeat the experience…

He had been to numerous breathtaking destinations during his lifetime, but never before had he ever felt the need to revisit any of them.

They took their time in the bath. It was a giant-sized bath, big enough to accommodate him comfortably. He could lie down and she could lie on top of him, her back against his torso, their knees protruding through the bubbles. She could feel him pressing against her, could know exactly how aroused he was, and he in turn could explore every inch of her wet body with his hands, soaping and massaging and generally working them both up to a state of maddening arousal.

His mind drifted back to the suggestion of a holiday with her, back to the island. Or they could go somewhere else. She had been abroad, apparently, as a child—presumably before her father had disappeared—but as an adult she had taken lamentably few holidays. He couldn't quite figure out why that would be when she was so highly paid and could have afforded some pretty good holidays abroad—if not twice a year, then at least once.

He could take her to Paris. Rome. Venice. All three. Or they could go further afield. Mauritius. The Maldives. Some other exotic destination where he could savour her delight and enjoy every new experience with her through fresh eyes. It was an appealing thought.

He would talk to her later, feel out the ground. She was

remarkably independent and he certainly didn't want that to change—certainly didn't want to introduce any element to their relationship other than transitory.

And yet…

They finally emerged from the bath. Standing in front of the mirror, he could watch her reflection—watch as she towelled herself dry, ending up with her hair, which she rough-dried before running her fingers through it, trying to disentangle the knots.

She caught his eye and grinned. 'Your phone's going again.'

Leandro took his time. When he finally made it to his mobile it had stopped ringing and there was a voicemail message to pick up from the guy he had not expected to hear back from so soon. Only hours after instructions had been given. Money certainly bought speed.

In the bathroom, doing something about her hair, Emily was unaware that Leandro had left the bedroom. She dressed, dabbed on some make-up, and when after half an hour he'd failed to reappear she headed down to the kitchen, where he was most likely to be.

His apartment was more of a townhouse than a flat, and spanned three floors of unadulterated luxury. She had become quickly accustomed to the display of wealth and now she bypassed the paintings, the handmade furniture and mirrors, the wood and marble, until she ended up in the kitchen to find him staring out through the French doors with his back to her.

He didn't turn around when she walked up behind him. 'Everything okay?'

Leandro turned slowly to look at her. He had changed into casual clothes and had his hands shoved deep into his pockets. His hair was still damp and was swept back from his face.

'There's a guy who works for me,' Leandro said expressionlessly. 'His name's Alberto. I use him when I want sensitive information unearthed. He's not high-profile in the company but he's a key member of my team and he's very good at what he does.'

'Why are you telling me this?'

'Because I had him do a few background checks on your ex-fiancé...'

'You did *what*...?' Emily made her way to a chair and sat heavily.

'Well might you look as white as a ghost.'

'You had no right!'

'You're my woman. I had every right, considering the circumstances surrounding this relationship of ours, and I can tell that you're just dying to find out what my private investigator told me... Or maybe you have an idea... Yes, I'm guessing you do have an idea...'

'I know you're going to jump to all the wrong conclusions,' Emily muttered.

'I've heard of marrying for security, Emily, but you really take the biscuit, don't you?'

His voice was neutral but he could feel pure rage coursing through his veins like poison. This was the woman who had obsessed him to such an extent that he had actually considered going on holiday with her! A woman who had cast such a powerful spell that for the first time in his life work had become a secondary consideration! He had spent so long thinking with the wrong part of his body that the reality of what had been happening under his nose was a bitter pill to swallow.

Even worse was the fact that as she sat there, staring up at him with those big cornflower-blue eyes, his body was *still* letting him down!

'I finally understand why you did what you did. Why

you launched yourself into a relationship with me when there was some sad sack in the background, waiting for you to show up at the aisle. Because a gay husband doesn't require fidelity, *does* he?'

Emily shook her head mutely.

'You were marrying your gay friend because you felt safe with him. Your father had instilled in you a belief that you were never to trust a man, but you *could* trust a man who would never take advantage of you. You could marry someone for affection because it was better than never getting married. Oh, and of course he came with a hefty bank balance... Maybe you figured that you didn't want to spend the rest of your life working hard but still never really being able to afford the best. Maybe you thought that a rich guy who could never threaten you on the physical front, who could never touch you enough to hurt you, was worth the sacrifice...'

Emily, her head lowered, didn't say anything. This was her big chance to fill in the missing blanks in the picture he was painting, but what would be the point? This wasn't a committed relationship in which she would fight for him. This was a one-sided relationship which was always going to see her being the mug who got hurt.

And he had got so much right, at any rate...

'So?' Leandro prompted impatiently. 'Have you nothing to say?'

He raked frustrated fingers through his hair and glowered at her from a distance. Naturally what they had was well and truly over, but the thought of her exiting in a shroud of silence filled him with impotent rage.

'Shall I continue telling you what I think the ending to this story is?' he thundered, making her jump and forcing her to look at him as he strode towards her and planted himself directly in her line of vision.

'Do I have a choice?'

Leandro turned away. He could *feel* her, and it put him off his stride. Now was not the time to have any lapses in concentration.

'I think you figured that you could dump the security and hang on to me for as long as you could. You know from first-hand experience how generous I am with my lovers…'

Emily's mouth dropped open and she stared at him in dismay. 'That's crazy,' she said, flabbergasted at his leap-frogging of information to reach the wrong conclusions.

And yet, how could she blame him? Her behaviour had not been straightforward. She had given him half-truths and the fewest possible details about Oliver she had been able to get away with. Naturally she had known what he would think had he discovered that her intended groom was gay—what *anyone* would think—and so she had concealed that small but glaringly important detail. How could she have said anything?

She looked at him helplessly and her blue eyes tangled with his hostile, cold, dark ones.

'I would never use…'

Wouldn't she? Use someone for money? Hadn't she done just that with Oliver? And even if it was by mutual agreement, did that make the slightest difference?

'I think I should go.' She hovered for the briefest of moments, willing him to beg her to stay. As if he would!

'Is that it?' Leandro heard the edge of what sounded like fury and frustration in his voice and hated the vulnerability that came with it.

'I'm not after your money.'

'Oh, please. I should have seen the warning signs. I once nearly got sucked in by someone of your kind—someone who did such a damn good job of pretending that I was almost conned into believing the woman wasn't a gold-digger.

To think I was nearly had again. The big blue eyes and the trembling mouth aren't going to cut it, darling. You can tell me till you're blue in the face that you weren't with me for the money—with sex, I'm sure, a nice bonus on the side—but face it… You don't deny that you were planning on marrying a guy who could never have fulfilled you physically because it was *convenient*…because he came with a nice, *convenient* bank balance…'

'Sometimes we do things that we may not particularly have mapped out for ourselves when we were young and idealistic…'

'You're still young!'

'But I dumped the ideals a long time ago!'

If only. She hadn't, had she? No, they had all been waiting there for the right guy to come along and turn her world upside down… For the right guy to hurt her.

She turned away, trembling. 'I'll go now,' she said stiffly.

Surprised, she realised that her hands were balled into tightly clenched fists and she slowly relaxed them and flexed her fingers.

'I don't want you to think the worst of me.' The plea was wrenched out of her.

'Then why don't you try telling me something to prevent that from happening!' Leandro stared at her and then flung his hands up in a gesture of enraged dismissal. 'I thought not! Well, Emily, it was always going to end. And you know where the door is…'

CHAPTER TEN

LEANDRO HEARD THE doorbell through a haze of too much alcohol. He had always made it a rule never to drink beyond a certain amount. He had been to far too many client events where the champagne had flowed and things had been said and done that were regretted in the cold light of day.

But five minutes after she had walked out of his house the bottle of wine had suddenly become his best friend.

He groggily looked at his watch, registering that it was after midnight and that he was still slumped in the chair in the sitting room where he had been for several hours, bar a couple of essential trips to the bathroom.

He heard the doorbell again, finger-on-buzzer-not-stopping-till-you-get-this style, and swore softly under his breath.

Emily. Who else? For a few seconds he contemplated not getting it, because there was nothing she had to say to him that could possibly alter his opinion of her. Nothing at all.

But he'd spent the past few hours drowning something or other in a bottle and why shouldn't she see it? He'd probably feel a damn sight better if he really offloaded on her! Really told her exactly what he thought about someone who had played him for a fool. He'd thought he could never be had again. He'd been wrong. Wouldn't it feel good to vent that anger and frustration?

He walked in a fairly straight line and yanked open the front door.

Emily, having chewed over the way they had parted company and made the brave decision to return to his house, stared at him in surprise.

'Are you *drunk*?'

His hair looked as though he had run his fingers through it a million times and his shirt was hanging loose over the waistband of his trousers. He was barefoot.

'What are you doing here?'

Was he *posturing? Defensive?* Neither option was cool and he scowled at her, noting in passing that she looked as fresh as a daisy despite the lateness of the hour.

'And how did you get here anyway?' He squinted to see if he could make out a taxi and couldn't.

'Tube and foot.'

'That's bloody crazy,' Leandro growled.

'Not as crazy…' Emily took a deep, fortifying breath and looked at him without blinking. 'Not as crazy as if I were to head back home by tube and foot, because there was a group of drunken teenagers outside the station, but that's what I'll do if you don't let me in.'

It was all bravado. She hoped he couldn't detect the desperate edge to her voice. Of course the outcome of this unexpected visit would change nothing, but she had had no choice but to come. To tell him everything. She didn't want, never mind *expect,* his sympathy, but she had finally come to the conclusion that love wasn't just painful, it also made a shambles of all your good intentions and put you in a place where you just could no longer forge ahead and think straight. You found yourself compelled to do things that went against the grain—compelled to ditch your pride, to become…vulnerable, whatever the consequences.

'You'd better come in, but I should warn you that you're

an uninvited guest and the only reason I'm not shutting the door on you is because I wouldn't send my worst enemy out at this hour, to face the vagaries of public transport.'

Leandro marvelled that he had managed that sentence without slurring his words. He began heading back towards the sitting room and could feel her presence behind him.

The lethargy that had afflicted him seemed to have miraculously disappeared.

'You should drink some black coffee—sober up.'

Leandro swung round to look at her and Emily automatically took a couple of steps back.

'Reason being...?'

'I don't want you falling all over the place when I say what I...I've come to say...'

'Why don't you tell me now and get it over and done with? I'm thinking you've had a chance to rustle up a plausible story, but you can forget it if you imagine that a plausible story can buy you a ticket back to my bed.'

'Do you know something, Leandro? I am mystified as to how I could have done something so stupid as to fall in love with you!'

Leandro stared at her. He didn't need any black coffee. He felt as sober as a judge. And once he'd started staring he found that he couldn't peel his eyes away from her face. She was bright red but she was standing her ground, glaring at him as though she had somehow been forced to utter those words against her will.

'I don't think I heard you correctly.'

'I'm in love with you. Okay?'

Leandro suddenly laughed, leaning against the wall. 'Nice try,' he finally said drily.

The cynicism he should have been feeling was curiously absent. Instead he was filled with a wild satisfaction which he could only put down to having had his ego stroked.

'What do you mean, *"nice try"*?'

'I mean you only jacked the ex in on the back of being able to sustain a relationship with me for as long as it would take to leave with some financial gain and you must be kicking yourself that you never quite managed to reach the point of success...'

In love with him? It was a bloody lie—of course it was. She had economised with the truth to such an extent that he would be a complete fool to believe a word she came out with. He should, he knew, just call her a cab and cut short this pointless conversation before it had time to degenerate into a shouting match. He didn't *do* shouting, or hitting things, but he had a suspicion that she was just the woman to bring that out in him.

Emily continued to glare, then she sidestepped him and headed towards the kitchen, not looking back to see if he was following her, knowing that he was. She was ramrod-straight, her head held high, but her heart was beating a mile a minute and she felt dizzy and sick.

The kitchen was a marvel of up-to-the-minute technology. It had never been her style and she had told him so on numerous occasions, much to his amusement, but she could still admire the stark lines, the clean surfaces and the plethora of high-tech gadgets, none of which looked as though they had ever been used.

There was an advanced and scary-looking coffee-making machine on the counter, sparkling white against the black granite, but she opted for the kettle instead and didn't look at him as she made them both some coffee. Black for him...white with two teaspoons of sugar for herself.

When she did finally turn around it was to see him lounging against the doorframe, watching her with narrow-eyed hostility.

'You should sit.'

'Who the hell do you think you are, Emily? Walking in here after we've parted company and issuing orders?'

'I think I'm a woman who never expected to fall in love with you, or with anyone, and now that I have I find that I can't walk away without…without telling you the whole story…'

'What's there to tell? You were going to marry a gay guy for his money before you decided that I was a better bet. No marriage needed and yet play your cards right, plenty of hot sex, and sooner or later—money…'

'Sit down, Leandro!'

How on earth was she managing to do this? She just knew that she had to lay the whole story on the line for him and then he could do with the information what he liked. Despise her more. Kick her out. Turn her into the butt of his jokes in the years to come. Whatever…

Leandro opened his mouth to protest in automatic dismissal of anyone daring to tell him what to do. Except… hadn't he dumped that all-controlling persona with her?

He shrugged nonchalantly and moved to one of the black leather chairs, turning it away from the chrome and glass table so that he was looking at her.

'Okay.' Emily drew in a deep breath. 'I got engaged to Oliver knowing that he was gay because it suited us both.'

She took a few seconds to get her thoughts into order, to arrange them in a way that made some kind of sense. Hesitantly, she walked across to the table and sat facing him, nursing the mug between her hands.

'You wanted his money,' Leandro said with scathing contempt.

'I wanted his money,' Emily agreed. 'I *needed* his money.'

Her blue eyes were clear and honest when she looked at him, and Leandro did his best to fight the temptation to be

sucked into whatever fairytale she was telling even though
he knew that what he would hear would be the full truth,
no holds barred.

About time. Lord only knew what she was going to come
out with. A secret gambling addiction? Debts that had been
racked up to the point of no return?

'*Needed*?'

'I told you about my father—about what he had done.
What I didn't tell you was that when he took off for Bangkok he took all the money with him. Mum tried to get some
kind of settlement but she waited too long, was too dazed
by what had happened. During that time he made as much
of his money disappear as he could. By the time the lawyers demanded full financial disclosure he was claiming
poverty and announcing that he was broke.'

Emily had been young at the time, but she could still
remember her mother wondering how on earth they were
going to afford to live, to put bread on the table.

'She had to go out to work to make ends meet. We lived
in the family home. A mansion. It had been in my mother's
family for generations and she refused to get rid of it even
though it ate money. In winter whole sections had to be
shut off because we couldn't begin to afford to run them.'

'What exactly *did* your mother manage to get from the
guy?'

'My father?' Emily sighed. 'A pittance. I had to be pulled
from private school, and that was that for holidays. Anyway, all my dreams of a career basically went down the
pan because I simply had to go out to work and get a good
job—which I did as fast as I could. By then Mum had been
ill for a while. Breast cancer. I believe it was brought on
by the stress.'

'I'm sorry,' Leandro said gruffly. 'Why didn't you say

something before? And what does this have to do with the gay fiancé?'

He had to return the conversation to a point he could handle.

'I'm getting there,' Emily said quietly. 'My mother has early onset Alzheimer's. It's not serious. But it's going to get worse. Eventually she's going to need proper care, but she still refuses to sell the house and I can't afford to cover the costs on my salary. As it is, most of what I earn goes towards helping her and keeping the wretched house from falling into complete disrepair.'

She ran her fingers through her hair and realised that her hand was trembling.

'I reconnected with Oliver a while ago. He'd been in the States and made a small fortune. He had a proposal for me. He wanted to get his foot back on the ground over here. Property. He had grand schemes for a golf course. Our house sits in a lot of land—most of it wild, wooded. You know... He knows the house well, and the land, and he suggested that if we got married I could sign the house over to him and he would help keep it ticking over. When the time came, in exchange for the house—which he would turn into a high-end country hotel set in its own private golf course—he would give me a sum of money sufficient to give my mother the best possible private care available and to set me up in my own little place. He was willing to bide his time, and figured that he would be able to get in with the small community by being my husband. He didn't think that they would accept him if he came out. It suited me.'

She looked at him defiantly, challenging him to criticise the decision she had taken.

'Everything wrapped up in a neat, sexless package...'

'I couldn't have agreed to it otherwise,' Emily admitted frankly. 'I may not have believed in love or romance, or the value of marriage, but there was no way that I could have had a sexual relationship with someone who was involved with me just as a business deal, so to speak. And then...'

There was no mistaking the sincerity on her face and Leandro could feel a weight beginning to lift from his shoulders. Believing the worst in her had been painful, and now he knew why.

'And then we went to the island and I just couldn't resist *you*...Leandro.' She laughed wryly. 'You were the last man on the planet I would ever have considered a suitable guy, and yet maybe that made my decision to sleep with you easier. You see...I'd never been attracted to anyone the way I was attracted to you. It was like my sensible, practical, cynical self had decided to take a holiday and the new occupants of the house had turned out to be wild, unruly and utterly out of control...'

Leandro was smiling. He wanted to whistle. His soul was soaring.

'It's not funny,' Emily muttered, looking at him with suspicion, because this was *not* in the repertoire of his reactions she had predicted.

'I'm sorry. Carry on. You had just got to the bit where you couldn't resist me...'

Emily cringed inwardly but she got it. She had lied and he had every right to enjoy each morsel of truth leaving her mouth.

'When I decided to break off with Oliver I did it because I knew that I had fallen in love with you, and the thought of getting married because it made sense on a number of practical fronts was just no longer conceivable.' She draped her hair over one shoulder and fiddled with the ends. 'The last thing I was after was any money. I'd already resigned myself to just doing the best I could with what I earned and crossing bridges when I came to them. Because I knew that you and I were never going to last. I knew what you wanted was sex—that you were still looking for the dream girl to provide you with the dream life.'

'Why didn't you tell me the whole truth when you broke off the engagement with your fiancé?' It felt okay for him to nurture magnanimous feelings towards the dearly and now departed ex.

'Because I knew what you'd think. That I had no morals. Who would sacrifice their lives for the sake of money?'

'Except you weren't doing that, really, were you?' Leandro said softly. 'I would have seen someone willing to sacrifice the happiness she didn't think she believed in for the sake of the mother she loved very much. I would have seen a woman willing to accept friendship as a basis for marriage because of altruistic reasons. I would have seen the woman I had fallen in love with.'

It was Emily's turn to stare at him. She wondered whether she had heard right. His expression was soft and intense and open all at the same time, and her mouth went dry because she didn't want to misread anything.

'Have I rendered you speechless?'

'I'm not sure I heard correctly,' she said faintly.

'Then I'll repeat it, because one good confession deserves another, don't you think? I love you. I love you and I didn't even realise it. I wasn't looking for love and I therefore assumed that it wouldn't arrive. God, Emily…' He shook his head and remembered the feelings earlier that had driven him to the bottle. 'When you left today I thought I was going out of my mind. It felt like a part of me had been ripped out, and even then I managed to convince myself that it was because I hadn't taken you for a liar, because I was annoyed, disappointed, angry…'

Emily reached across the table and her hands found his.

They linked fingers. She felt the energy run between them—familiar, exciting and comforting all at the same time.

'You're really telling me that you love me…?'

'You were cynical and didn't believe in love. I was fully committed to the idea, but on my terms and within my control and at a time that slotted in to my schedule. I guess it's fair to say that you weren't the only one to be taken by surprise…'

He stood up, pulling her to her feet and drawing her into him.

'I love you, Emily Edison, and I would like to know if you could take me on—for better or for worse…'

'Are you asking what I think you're asking?'

'Depends… I'm asking you to marry me.'

'You would think that I want your money if I said yes…'

'I would think that you wouldn't have a choice but to let me help you, because that's what people do when they love each other.'

'I…'

'Yes or no?'

Emily smiled. She grinned until her jaw began to ache and she squeezed him tightly, barely daring to breathe in case the moment was broken.

'Yes!'

'You agree to take me on, for better or for worse.'

'For better or for worse…'

'And my worse is that I update that pile of yours so that your mother is happy and comfortable for ever in the place she loves and the place you love too—because I will always love what you love, my darling…'

He drew her apart and brushed some hair away from her forehead.

'I don't know what I would have done if you hadn't shown up here tonight,' he said quietly. 'I would have come to find you, but my pride would have made me take my time, and I shudder with fear to think about what you might have done in the interim. Reconsidered your options about marrying the ex…' He felt sick when he thought about it.

'Never…' She stroked his cheek and kissed the side of his mouth, smiling as she felt the shift inside him as his libido kicked in as effortlessly as hers did. 'You've spoiled me for the rest of the opposite sex…'

'And you'd better keep it that way…'

He held her hand and began leading her out of the kitchen, back up to the bedroom, where he had every intention of sealing their love in bed.

'And I shall keep reminding you on a daily basis how to do that…beginning, my love, with right now…'

* * * * *

MILLS & BOON®

Why not subscribe?

Never miss a title and save money too!

Here's what's available to you if you join the exclusive **Mills & Boon Book Club** today:

- ✦ *Titles up to a month ahead of the shops*
- ✦ *Amazing discounts*
- ✦ *Free P&P*
- ✦ *Earn Bonus Book points that can be redeemed against other titles and gifts*
- ✦ *Choose from monthly or pre-paid plans*

Still want more?

Well, if you join today we'll even give you
50% OFF your first parcel!

So visit **www.millsandboon.co.uk/subs**
or call Customer Relations on **020 8288 2888**
to be a part of this exclusive Book Club!

SUBS_2014